Sarah Morgan is a rising star in
Harlequin Presents® and we hope
that you'll continue to enjoy her stories....

Sarah's intense, dramatic and passionate
stories will take you on a roller
coaster of emotions!

"Sarah Morgan [creates] a dynamic
and intense read."
—*Romantic Times*

SARAH MORGAN trained as a nurse and
has since worked in a variety of health-related
jobs. Married to a gorgeous businessman who still
makes her knees knock, she spends most of
her time trying to keep up with their two little
boys, but manages to sneak off occasionally
to indulge her passion for writing romance. Sarah
loves outdoor life and is an enthusiastic skier
and walker. Whatever she is doing, her head is
always full of new characters and she is addicted
to happy endings.

Proud, passionate, primal—
Dare she surrender to the sheikh?
Find rapture in the sands in
Harlequin Presents®

Look out for more stories of passion
under the dry desert sun, coming soon!

Next month:

Favorite author Penny Jordan revisits the
kingdom of Zuran for the final installment
of her Arabian Nights saga:
Possessed by the Sheikh
#2457

Coming in June:
The Sheikh's Virgin
by Jane Porter
#2473

Sarah Morgan

IN THE SHEIKH'S MARRIAGE BED

Surrender To The Sheikh

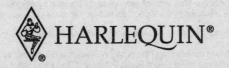

HARLEQUIN®

TORONTO • NEW YORK • LONDON
AMSTERDAM • PARIS • SYDNEY • HAMBURG
STOCKHOLM • ATHENS • TOKYO • MILAN • MADRID
PRAGUE • WARSAW • BUDAPEST • AUCKLAND

If you purchased this book without a cover you should be aware that this book is stolen property. It was reported as "unsold and destroyed" to the publisher, and neither the author nor the publisher has received any payment for this "stripped book."

ISBN 0-373-12453-8

IN THE SHEIKH'S MARRIAGE BED

First North American Publication 2005.

Copyright © 2004 by Sarah Morgan.

All rights reserved. Except for use in any review, the reproduction or utilization of this work in whole or in part in any form by any electronic, mechanical or other means, now known or hereafter invented, including xerography, photocopying and recording, or in any information storage or retrieval system, is forbidden without the written permission of the publisher, Harlequin Enterprises Limited, 225 Duncan Mill Road, Don Mills, Ontario, Canada M3B 3K9.

All characters in this book have no existence outside the imagination of the author and have no relation whatsoever to anyone bearing the same name or names. They are not even distantly inspired by any individual known or unknown to the author, and all incidents are pure invention.

This edition published by arrangement with Harlequin Books S.A.

® and TM are trademarks of the publisher. Trademarks indicated with ® are registered in the United States Patent and Trademark Office, the Canadian Trade Marks Office and in other countries.

www.eHarlequin.com

Printed in U.S.A.

PROLOGUE

'YOUR orders have been carried out, Your Highness—the debt to your people has been repaid in full.'

Staring out of the window of his office, Zak dragged his gaze away from his favourite Arab stallion who was causing havoc in the yard below.

Cold anger shimmered in his night-black eyes as he surveyed the man who had been his most trusted aide for almost two decades. 'Not quite in full. The debt owed to me still stands. Was everything delivered to the Englishman?'

The man swallowed and bowed his head. 'As instructed, Your Highness—'

Zak detected something in the other man's tone and instantly his gaze sharpened. 'He is attending the meeting, Sharif?'

Sharif paled slightly. 'I have been informed that he is sending his sister in his place,' he offered hesitantly, stepping backwards as he saw the flash of raw anger in the prince's eyes.

So the Englishman had once again avoided his responsibilities, Zak mused grimly, flexing his broad shoulders in an attempt to release the mounting tension in his powerful frame. Sometimes he wished that Kazban were not such a progressive state. At times like this he would dearly love to return to his primitive, tribal roots and dispense the punishment that Peter Kingston so richly deserved.

Sharif cleared his throat. 'Given the nature of the meeting, it is a somewhat surprising decision on his part. One wonders what sort of man sends a woman to fight his battles?'

'A coward.' Zak's hard mouth tightened. By refusing to travel to Kazban, the Englishman had cleverly avoided being

5

held accountable for his actions. 'But then we already knew that Peter Kingston is a coward. So it hardly comes as that much of a surprise that he is prepared to sacrifice his own flesh and blood in an attempt to save his own skin. He is sending her into the lions' den. I hope she is wearing armour.'

His chief adviser cleared his throat delicately. 'He is doubtless hoping that you will show her leniency,' he ventured and Zak gave a bitter laugh.

Had Peter Kingston known anything of his past then he wouldn't have made such a serious error of judgment. His feelings towards the female sex were anything but gentle and forgiving. Life had taught him in the most brutal way possible that all women were manipulative and self-seeking and since learning that lesson he now treated them with the cynical contempt they deserved.

His dark eyes hardened. 'The man is little more than a thief, although I admit a clever one. He has stolen the savings of innocent, hard working citizens. In his country that may be considered acceptable behaviour, but in Kazban fortunately we are not so foolish. In this instance I feel no inclination towards leniency.'

Sharif clasped his hands in front of him. 'It is true that his actions would have caused untold hardship for many had it not been for your generous intervention, Your Highness. In my opinion your people should know that it is *you* who has—'

'That is not important.' Zak interrupted him, a frown touching his black brows as he paced the full length of his office, his tread muffled by the beautifully woven rug that covered the floor of the room. 'What is important is that we send a clear message to others who might be tempted to follow the same dishonest course as Kingston. Clearly he anticipated reprisals and this is the reason that he has chosen not to attend the meeting himself. He is not only dishonest but he takes no responsibility for his own actions.' His tone was contemptuous. 'I intend to make an example of him.'

Sharif took a deep breath. 'Sending his sister in his place is a clever move on his part. It is no secret that you enjoy the company of women, Your Highness,' he offered tactfully and Zak's eyes narrowed.

'In my bed, Sharif,' he said softly, his arrogant dark head lifting slightly as he surveyed his trusted adviser. 'Outside my bed, women have no place in my life.'

He would never, ever trust a woman again.

Sharif shifted slightly, his sharp gaze suddenly sympathetic. 'And yet your father is becoming more and more insistent that you marry, Your Highness.'

Zak gritted his teeth. 'I am well aware of my father's wishes,' he said coldly and Sharif sighed.

'You will doubtless say that I am exceeding my responsibilities,' he ventured hesitantly, 'but as one who has known and loved you from a boy, it saddens me to see you alone when you should be settled with a family.'

'As you rightly say, you exceed your responsibilities.' Zak's tone remained icy but his dark gaze softened slightly as they rested on the older man. His adviser was one of the few people whom he would trust with his life. 'Do not waste your emotions, Sharif. It is my choice to be alone but I'm well aware that my single status is becoming a thorn in my father's side.'

And he was going to have to address the issue.

But not by marrying the woman that his father had in mind.

When the time came—and he was grimly aware that the time was upon him—he would select his own bride and his choice would be made totally without sentiment.

His hard mouth tightened. 'Returning to the subject of Miss Kingston—'

Sharif shook his head regretfully. 'I'm sure the Englishman believes that you would never hurt a woman.'

Zak gave a slow smile, but there was no trace of amusement in his handsome features and when he spoke, his voice was dangerously soft. 'There is more than one type of pain, Sharif.' There was the pain of love. *And there was the white-hot agony of betrayal.* 'We both know that any woman connected to Peter Kingston is hardly likely to be coated in virtue. If he chooses to send a woman into battle, hoping that I won't have the stomach for a fight, then he's going to be disappointed.'

He turned his head and his gaze rested on the ceremonial sword that lay across his desk. Reaching out a hand, he lifted it, his long fingers closing over the ornate handle, the weight of the weapon both comforting and familiar in the palm of his hand.

His eyes traced the length of the deadly blade and a violent rush of emotions threatened to disturb his usually iron self-control.

Betrayal.

With a swift, athletic movement of his wrist he moved and the deadly blade sliced through the air with lethal accuracy.

Sharif took a hasty step backwards.

Like everyone else in the state of Kazban, he knew the extent of the prince's skill with that particular weapon. His Highness was an expert swordsman.

The woman had better be strong, Sharif thought, feeling an inexplicable sympathy for her as he watched the prince carefully replace the weapon on the desk, his handsome face hard and unforgiving. If Peter Kingston had wanted to cross someone, then he had made a very poor choice with Crown Prince Sheikh Zakour al-Farisi.

A very poor choice indeed.

CHAPTER ONE

'HIS HIGHNESS will see you now, Miss Kingston. You will remain standing at all times and speak only when you are spoken to.' Stern-faced and unsmiling, the man in robes bowed his head slightly, his eyes suddenly wary. 'I should warn you that His Highness is a busy man. There are many demands on him and he bears much responsibility. For your own sake I advise you not to waste his time.'

Emily swallowed hard, suddenly questioning the impulse that had made her volunteer to take her brother's place.

She'd wanted to help.

To do something for *him*, for a change, instead of always being in the role of little sister.

Peter had done so much for her—

And she'd thought that a few days in Kazban would be exciting. An adventure in her otherwise boring, overprotected existence. But she was beginning to doubt her abilities to carry out the task in hand.

She was beginning to wonder whether her presence might make things worse for him.

Whichever way you looked at it, Crown Prince Zakour al-Farisi was *not* going to like what she had to say.

Her brother owed him money. That was why the prince had ordered this meeting.

And the way things stood at the moment, Peter wasn't in a position to pay.

'If I go, Em, I'll be thrown into jail.'

At the time she'd thought that her brother was exaggerating. Surely the state of Kazban couldn't be that brutal in its laws? Coming on behalf of her brother to beg for more

9

time had seemed a perfectly reasonable and straightforward action when she'd been in England.

But now she was here, she wasn't so sure—

And the severe expression on the face of the prince's adviser wasn't doing anything for her confidence.

Forcing herself to stay calm, she rose to her feet, trying to forget the little she'd heard about the next ruler of the state of Kazban. So what if the man had a brilliant mind, amused himself with scores of women and was reputed to have a block of ice where his heart was supposed to be? None of it was of any relevance to her. She really didn't care that half the women in the world were supposedly in love with the man.

All she had to do was deliver her brother's message and then leave.

But what if she said the wrong thing?

It was all very well dreaming about adventure but the truth was that she taught five year olds to read and write and play nicely in the playground. She had no idea how to talk to a man who negotiated billion dollar deals before breakfast. Her brother must have been mad to allow her to come.

Or desperate.

She couldn't shake the feeling that Peter was in some sort of trouble. When she'd tried to question him about the debt, he'd assured her that he just had a slight cash-flow problem that would soon be sorted out and that there was nothing for her to worry about.

But hadn't he always protected her?

Remembering just how tense her brother had seemed the last time they'd met, she suddenly wished she'd questioned him more.

Her heart thudding painfully in her chest, she followed the man down what seemed like miles of marble corridor, trying not to feel intimidated by the glittering, exotic interior of the Golden Palace of Kazban. At any other time her inquisitive teacher's mind would have been buzzing with questions relating to the history of this ancient building but the sight of armed guards in almost every doorway squashed her natural curiosity.

Telling herself that the guards were there because this was the home of the royal family, she averted her eyes from the guns and swords. They were just part of the uniform. And she had no reason to feel uneasy. No reason at all.

She was simply the messenger.

So why did part of her suddenly want to turn and run?

Run back through the dusty streets of Kazban, back through the mysterious, sun-baked desert that she'd been driven through on the way from the airport, back home to the tiny English village where she lived.

Back to loneliness—

She pushed the thought away quickly. She had a job to do. For the first time in her life, her brother needed her and she wasn't going to let him down. Not after everything he'd done for her since their parents had died.

Emily struggled to keep pace with the man who had collected her from the entrance to the palace. 'Could you slow down a bit, please? I only brought one pair of shoes with me and they're not suitable for sprinting on marble floors,' she muttered, wondering where they were going. 'I don't want to see the prince with a broken ankle.'

In fact she'd just decided that she didn't actually want to see the prince at all—

The man glanced at her with something that looked like pity in his eyes and Emily felt sicker and sicker.

All her instincts were telling her that this had been a bad, bad decision.

Why was everyone so afraid of Zak al-Farisi?

Was he really as heartless and ruthless as his reputation suggested?

Reminding herself firmly that there was good in everyone, she fought a battle with the panic that was threatening to swamp her.

The man stopped outside a door flanked by yet more guards and then entered, indicating that she should follow.

The panic suddenly won the battle.

'You know, I'm not sure about this. It's really my brother who should be here. If the prince is that busy then maybe I should just go home—' she said hopefully and then broke off, hustled by the man into yet another enormous room.

She stopped dead and her mouth fell open as she gazed around her in stunned amazement.

The room was beautiful. And exotic.

Light shone in from the numerous curved windows, illuminating an exquisite tapestry that hung on the far wall of the room.

'Oh—!' Intrigued, Emily peered closer, her eyes taking in every tiny detail. It depicted a horse race and for a moment she stood still, enchanted by the wildness of the horses and the life that pulsed from the tapestry. It was so skilfully woven that Emily could almost hear the thud of hooves and the snort of animals caught up in the excitement of the race.

Her awed gaze slid from the tapestry to the low sofas that nestled in one corner of the room, upholstered in gold silk and piled with layers of cushions in rich colours.

In the other corner of the room was an enormous desk, elaborately carved and providing a home for a state-of-the-art computer.

The contrast between the exotic and the functional made Emily blink. Whoever occupied this room obviously used it as an office.

She glanced round her and suddenly wished that she'd worn something different. The blue linen dress she'd chosen was cool and practical but it certainly wasn't the latest designer fashion. But then her teacher's income didn't exactly fund an elaborate wardrobe and because she worked with small children most of her clothes were chosen for practicality rather than style.

'Excuse me.' She tried one more time to communicate

with the man. 'Can you tell me when I'm going to meet the prince? You know, if he's really that busy perhaps I should just go—'

Maybe there was still time to get out of this. She could phone Peter and tell him that she'd changed her mind.

Instead of answering the man dropped to his knees on the beautifully woven rug, leaving her to stare at him in astonishment.

'You wish to leave, Miss Kingston?' A dry voice came from directly behind her. 'Is our hospitality really so lacking that the moment you arrive in our country, you suddenly wish to leave it? Or is something else fuelling this desire for flight? The knowledge that your sins are about to catch up with you, perhaps?'

'Sins?' She whirled round to face the speaker and felt her eyes lock with those of a stranger.

Her mouth dried and her heart started to bump heavily against her chest.

She was held prisoner by the force of that hard gaze, the lethal glitter in his dark eyes holding her captive. Intense sexual awareness ripped through her and she ceased to breathe. She felt light-headed and shaky, her whole body reacting with such shockingly powerful excitement that she couldn't move or think. It was only when he finally strolled forward that she was able to free herself from his grip.

He must have been standing there when she'd entered, but she'd been so overwhelmed by her surroundings that she'd failed to notice him.

How? she wondered helplessly. How had she failed to notice him? He dominated the room with his powerful presence, strolling across the room with a cool authority that couldn't be ignored.

If ever a man was designed to tempt a woman to stray from the straight and narrow, it was this one. He was dressed in a superbly tailored suit, his appearance conventional enough at first glance. But despite the outward display of

Western sophistication, she would never have placed him in the traditional confines of a business institution. Had she been asked to choose a setting for him, she would have placed him on the ocean as a pirate.

Or in the desert.

His looks and his presence matched the wildness of the landscape that she'd passed on her way to Kazban.

Everything about him was blatantly, savagely masculine from the gleaming jet-black hair smoothed back from his tanned brow to the perfect symmetry of his staggeringly handsome face. His nose was strong and aristocratic and his shoulders broad and powerful.

He was shockingly, *breathtakingly* handsome and Emily felt her limbs weaken.

Dizzy from lack of air and shaken by her own uncharacteristic response, she sucked in several breaths and tried to pull herself together while the man who had brought her to the room scrambled to his feet and shot her a black look.

'You should bow in the presence of the prince,' he hissed and she looked at him in confusion.

'The prince? Well, I will, of course, but—' She broke off as understanding dawned and hot colour flooded her cheeks. 'Oh, my goodness—'

She swallowed and bowed quickly, trying to rectify her mistake, painfully aware of that glittering dark gaze following her every move.

She should have guessed, of course. He was much younger than she'd expected and dressed in Western style, but power throbbed from every line of his impressive physique and everything about him shrieked of royalty. His carriage, his manner and the slightly cynical gleam in his midnight black eyes.

'I—I'm sorry—' She stammered her apology awkwardly and bowed her head again to be on the safe side. 'But you are partly to blame. You don't dress like a prince and you didn't introduce yourself.'

There was a muffled sound of alarm and disbelief from the man who had led her to the room but the prince's cool gaze didn't flicker.

'And how am I supposed to dress, Miss Kingston?' he enquired smoothly and Emily shivered as his deep, masculine voice slid over her bones like melted chocolate. He had the blazing self-confidence of someone who'd been on the receiving end of female adoration for his entire life.

'Well like—like—an Arabian prince,' she finished lamely. 'You know—robes and things…' Her voice tailed off and she closed her eyes briefly and cringed slightly. She sounded *so* stupid.

The prince obviously thought so too if his sardonic expression was anything to go by. 'Do you think this is some sort of pantomime,' he observed silkily, one dark eyebrow lifting in mockery, 'and that we should all be in costume?'

Without waiting for her reply he turned to the man who had been listening to the exchange with undisguised horror and snapped out a few words of a strange language.

The man made a hasty retreat, throwing pitying looks at Emily on the way out.

'I—I'm sorry for the confusion, Your Highness,' she mumbled, her cheeks burning with mortification.

How could she have made such a stupid mistake?

'There was no confusion on my part, Miss Kingston.'

He strode over to the window and stared down into the courtyard, momentarily distracted by something that was happening below him.

Emily just stared.

He was *spectacular*. Her eyes fixed on those thick dark lashes, slid down the hard planes of his handsome face to rest on his darkened jaw, before sliding down still further to the bulk of his shoulders.

Why were only half the women in the world in love with him? she wondered dizzily. What was the matter with the other half? Were they blind?

Or were they wise?

Suddenly aware that she was staring danger in the face for the first time in her boring, sheltered life, she took an involuntary step backwards, trying to shake off the shockingly hot thoughts that crowded her brain.

Appalled and confused by her own feelings, she hoped fervently that the man couldn't read minds.

'You must be wondering why I'm here—'

The prince turned suddenly, the expression in his eyes so chilly that she literally shivered.

'I have not invited you to speak.'

Emily's blue eyes widened in consternation and hot colour flooded her cheeks. Then she gave a little frown, dragging her eyes away from that cold gaze and telling herself that *whoever* he was, it didn't give him the right to be rude.

Her eyes fixed on his broad shoulders and she wondered helplessly why on earth he bothered with guards. He looked as though he could take on an entire army single-handed if the whim so took him. His suit was beautifully cut but there was no disguising the width of his shoulders or the muscles of his long, powerful thighs.

He was the very embodiment of masculine perfection and she felt her mouth dry as his arrogant gaze slid over her in a leisurely appraisal.

'Come closer,' he ordered harshly and she found herself obeying without question, almost hypnotized by the force of his presence.

At five feet ten she was used to staring most men directly in the eye and she just *hated* the fact that she was so tall, but standing face to face with this man she had to tip her head back to look at him. For the first time in her life she felt delicate and feminine and she found herself struggling to breathe, swamped by his overpowering masculinity.

'So.' He stood with his legs spread apart and his head thrown back, each sweep of that arrogant gaze draining her fragile confidence. 'For your sake, Miss Kingston, I hope that you are here to repay your brother's debt.'

There was something in his tone that made Emily wish fervently that she'd stayed in England.

'I'm not exactly repaying it *today*,' she began and his mouth tightened ominously.

'And yet that was the purpose of this meeting. Your brother was to repay the money owed.'

She gazed into those hard black eyes, searching for a hint of softness or compromise. Finding none, she licked her lips, suddenly finding it hard to speak. 'Well, it isn't quite as simple as that.'

'It is precisely as simple as that.'

How could a man's voice be so quiet and yet be filled with such menace?

No wonder he had a reputation for being a staggeringly successful businessman, Emily thought weakly. He probably intimidated his opponent so effectively that no one ever dared say 'no' to him.

'You're obviously wondering why I'm here instead of my brother,' she began hesitantly and his dark eyes gleamed with mockery.

'I am not a fool, Miss Kingston,' he said silkily, 'and it is entirely clear to me why you are here instead of your brother.'

His gaze slid over her in a blatantly masculine appraisal and suddenly she felt hot all over. He didn't actually need to speak to intimidate her. Just a look from those dangerous black eyes was enough to turn her legs wobbly.

'He sent me because he couldn't come himself,' Emily muttered, feeling a sudden urge to clarify that fact just in case he thought—*he thought*—

Zak al-Farisi lifted a dark eyebrow. 'My command of English is sufficiently advanced that I know the difference between "couldn't" and "wouldn't",' he drawled. 'I am intrigued as to which one of your many and varied charms were supposed to soothe my anger at your brother's absence. Which one of your skills is guaranteed to take my mind off the debt, I wonder?'

Moving away from the window, he paced towards her, walking around her as if she were an exhibit in a museum, a predatory smile on his handsome face. He paused and lifted a hand to her face, tilting it slightly so that he could study her more closely. 'Your purpose here is to persuade me to cancel the debt.'

'Not *cancel* exactly—' Emily was finding it difficult to concentrate, frozen to the spot by a tension that she couldn't identify and by the touch of his strong fingers against her hot cheek '—more *postpone*.'

His hard mouth tightened. 'Before you dig yourself deep into a hole from which there is no escape, you should know that deception is not a quality I admire in a woman.'

'I am not deceiving anyone,' Emily said indignantly, 'and I'm not asking you to cancel the debt. Just to give Peter more time. He wants two more months. Then he'll pay back every penny. He's given his word.'

'Is this the same word he gave when he first arrived in Kazban to persuade us to let him handle certain investments?'

Her heart missed a beat and she shifted uncomfortably. The truth was that her brother always refused to discuss business with her and she certainly wasn't in a position to answer in depth questions. She was only here to help her brother; he couldn't make the trip and because she loved him—she was happy to represent him.

'I don't know anything about that,' she admitted reluctantly, 'but I do know that all he's asking for is two months.'

Those pitch-black eyes lasered into hers. 'And why should I give him two months?'

Emily looked at him in confusion. It hadn't occurred to her that the prince would deny the request. True, Peter owed him money, but Zak al-Farisi was rich beyond fantasies so a two month extension on a tiny debt was hardly going to cause him a problem, was it?

She gave an uncertain smile. 'Well, I'm sure you're a nice guy—'

'Then you are a poor judge of character, Miss Kingston, because I am not a nice guy,' he delivered softly, his black eyes narrowing slightly as they raked her increasingly pale face. 'I'm not a nice guy at all.'

The air thickened with tension and then with his free hand he reached out and removed the clip from her hair in a swift, purposeful gesture that she didn't anticipate.

Her wayward blonde curls, so carefully tamed for this one meeting, tumbled down her back in glorious rebellion and shimmering black eyes fastened on her hair in blatant masculine appraisal.

'Oh!' She gave a gasp of dismay and clutched at her hair. 'What did you do that for?'

A sardonic smile touched his hard mouth. 'I told you that I don't appreciate deception. Presenting yourself here dressed like a virgin in a dress buttoned to your neck and your hair pinned back doesn't fool me in the slightest. Your brother sent you because of your feminine charms. The least you can do is to display them. That, at least, would be honest.'

Emily gaped at him.

He thought—

He was suggesting—

Aghast, she shook her head, one hand still on her tumbled curls that were now cascading freely over her shoulders. 'You've got it all wrong—'

'I don't think so. In fact I am finding myself forced to admit that your brother is evidently not the fool I believed him to be.' Having made that announcement, he dropped his hand and strolled around her, his gaze sweeping over her with embarrassing thoroughness. 'You are *very* beautiful.'

Beautiful?

Momentarily distracted by his surprising declaration, Emily stared at him.

He thought she was *beautiful*? Not just beautiful, but *very beautiful*.

Indoctrinated from adolescence into thinking that she was too tall to be considered beautiful, she struggled to breathe, trapped by the novelty of being on the receiving end of raw male appreciation for the first time in her life.

And then she saw something flicker in his eyes and reminded herself that this man didn't have a heart. He was refusing to give Peter more time and he seemed to think that she was offering herself as some sort of consolation prize.

From somewhere she found her voice, jerking away from him and smoothing her tumbled hair with shaking hands. 'I don't see how the way I dress has anything to do with this—'

'Do you not?' His hard mouth curved slightly. 'And yet you agreed to come here, Miss Kingston.'

He was standing so close that she could feel the heat throb between them, feel the tension rise to such a pitch that she could hardly breathe.

'I came to deliver my brother's message.'

He smiled. 'Consider it delivered. Now we can move on.'

Her cheeks flamed under his steady gaze. 'I don't know what you're implying,' she said frostily, 'but—'

'Miss Kingston—' his tone was lethally soft and he took a step closer to her, his eyes locking on hers with magnetic force, his powerful body dominating hers even though they weren't touching '—I ought to warn you that I never play games. Not in my business dealings or in my bedroom dealings.'

Emily flushed, wondering which category he thought she fell into. 'I'm not playing games, but you're tying me in knots and you're being so inflexible about the money—' She broke off, totally quelled by the contempt in those black eyes.

'I am not known for my flexibility.'

Or for warmth or kindness, Emily reflected. She'd never met anyone so cold and unapproachable in her life. He was totally intimidating and he was standing *so* close that she could almost feel the heat of his body burning through the thin fabric of her dress.

'My brother sends his apologies for not coming himself,' she said formally, raking a mass of blonde curls away from her eyes and suddenly wishing that she'd dug a little deeper and found out *exactly* why her brother hadn't been able to attend. *Had he known the prince would be this angry?* 'He's been working really hard and I agreed to come in his place, to explain.'

Night-black eyes settled on hers and Emily felt her heart beat faster. He might be heartless but he had truly amazing cheekbones. In fact he was gorgeous, she thought weakly, wondering how she was supposed to concentrate faced with all that rampant, pulsing masculinity.

Suddenly all she could think about was sex and she dragged her eyes away from his, just *mortified* by her own thoughts. What was the matter with her? She never thought about sex. She thought about love and marriage and babies, and of course sex was part of that, but she never thought about *sex on its own.*

Until now.

There was something about Zak al-Farisi that was so powerfully sexual that it took her breath away. She glanced around her again, half expecting to see desperate women pouring through every door of his palace and an unsettling thought occurred to her.

Did Arab princes still have harems?

She glanced at that cold, handsome face one more time and felt her knees weaken alarmingly.

If there was a vacancy in this man's harem then she was *definitely* applying.

Or maybe not. She couldn't think of anything more terrifying than being in this man's bed.

Or more exciting—

'So—' his voice was soft and slightly accented '—I confess I am intrigued. I await your explanation with almost unbearable anticipation.'

Roused from her fantasies by the raw bite of his sarcasm, Emily decided that there was probably a waiting list for the harem. A very long one. And she wasn't exactly qualified for the position. What she knew about sex could be written on a thong.

Realising that he was still waiting for an answer, she drew breath. 'There's nothing to justify,' she said, puzzled and disconcerted by the flash of anger she saw in the prince's eyes. 'The investments aren't doing well. He told me that much. But he anticipates that the markets will improve soon. In the meantime, he's just asking you to give him more time.'

Those black eyes showed not a flicker of warmth. 'We've already established that I'm not a nice guy, Miss Kingston. I won't be giving him more time.'

She frowned, refusing to believe that anyone could be that unsympathetic. 'But none of this is Peter's fault,' she said and Zak lifted one inky-black eyebrow, his expression sardonic.

'He is no longer responsible for his own business?'

Emily nibbled her lip. 'Well yes, of course he is, but—'

'He was not responsible for investing the money?'

'Yes, he was, but—'

'So why is none of it his fault?'

His eyes were hard and Emily lifted a shaking hand to her head, just hating every minute of the conversation. He was setting a trap for her and she was galloping into it head first. She loathed confrontation and had absolutely no experience of business negotiation.

'Investing money is always a risky business,' she ventured and Zak tilted his head in silent question.

'You are no doubt an expert?' His voice was silky soft and loaded with mockery and Emily coloured.

'N-no—of course not,' she stammered awkwardly, trying really hard to ignore the pounding of her heart and the warmth that was spreading through her body. 'Actually I teach small children—but Peter told me that the investments have under performed and that it just happens that way sometimes.' She curled her fingers into her palms. 'Please give him more time. Just two months. That's all.'

She gave a helpless shrug that was supposed to indicate that she was asking for very little, but the expression in those ebony eyes was forbidding.

'All?' The prince continued to watch her, his sudden stillness unnerving. 'In two months a family can starve, Miss Kingston.'

She stared at him, her mouth drying.

A family? What family? And why would they starve?

They were talking about a few investments, not a fortune.

Emily glanced around at her opulent surroundings wondering if she was missing something.

It was perfectly obvious that the prince was unlikely to starve any day soon.

The palace was amazing. From the first moment she'd set eyes on the golden domes and the honey-coloured stone she'd been enchanted. It was like something straight out of a fairy tale.

'T-two months isn't very long,' she suggested hesitantly and his jaw hardened.

'And yet to some it can seem like a lifetime.'

Feeling that she was definitely missing something, Emily clasped her hands in front of her and tried one more time. 'I know it's inconvenient, but Peter will deliver the money,' she said firmly and saw the prince's eyes narrow.

'Such loyalty is most commendable, Miss Kingston, but

I'm afraid I don't share your confidence in your brother's ability to pay back that which he has taken. Your presence here is proof of his intention to default on the debt.'

'No!' Emily was quick to defend her brother. 'Peter will pay back the money.'

'So why didn't he come here to tell me that himself?'

Emily licked dry lips, shivering under that icy gaze. She'd asked herself that same question repeatedly. 'He—is busy,' she said lamely and Zak gave a wry smile.

'Of course he is. Ripping people off is a full-time job.'

Emily gave a gasp of outrage, her shyness forgotten in the face of the insult to her brother. 'My brother is not ripping people off—he just needs more time.'

'And I am not prepared to give him time, Miss Kingston.'

'But that's totally unreasonable,' she blurted out before she could stop herself. 'What has Peter ever done to you?'

A dark eyebrow swooped upwards, his arrogant dark head lifted in challenge. 'You are questioning my decision?'

Emily flushed scarlet, realizing too late that obviously no one ever questioned Zak al-Farisi's decisions.

'Well, yes, I mean, no,' she amended hastily. 'It's just that Peter will pay you eventually, and I can't see why the money matters to you so much.'

Evidence of his staggering wealth was all around her.

Nothing he could say would ever convince her that he needed the money in a hurry.

'Can you not?' His tone was as hard as his gaze. 'Then your judgment merely confirms that you are as lacking in morals as your brother. You are prepared to see people suffer as a result of your actions.'

Emily dragged her eyes away from his handsome face, totally unable to see how he was likely to suffer.

How could a small sum of money matter so much to him?

How could anyone be so selfish?

The Crown Prince was obviously totally unreasonable when it came to matters of money.

'All right.' Deciding that there was no point in arguing with someone who clearly had superior skills in the art, she lifted her chin, anxious to get away from him before she stopped remembering that personality was more important than looks. 'So you won't give him more time. I'll make sure I pass on that message to Peter when I return home.'

She made a move towards the door but lean, bronzed fingers closed around her wrist and she was held in an iron grip.

The prince gave a grim smile. 'You won't be returning home, Miss Kingston. You chose to come in your brother's place and for the time being at least I intend to keep you. As insurance.'

There was a ghastly silence while she digested his words. 'Keep me?'

'Of course.' His black eyes met hers, his gaze unflinching and totally devoid of sympathy. 'I expected your brother, but you have offered yourself freely in his place. If your brother wants me to release you, then he must come here himself.'

Emily blinked. 'You're asking me to stay here?'

A ghost of a smile touched that hard mouth. '*Not* asking, Miss Kingston,' he drawled softly, releasing her wrist and pacing around her slowly, like a predator sizing up a potential prey and deciding whether it was worth the kill. 'It is my decision that you will stay here until such time as your brother comes in person.'

Emily gaped at him. 'I'm your *prisoner*?'

'I prefer the term ''guest'',' the prince replied, his voice silky smooth. 'For as long as it pleases me, you will remain in the palace.'

For as long as it pleases me—

The air throbbed with tension and Emily felt an inexplicable heat spread throughout her body.

Just exactly what form was this pleasure going to take?

'No! You can't do that.' Emily was so shocked that she

forgot protocol for a moment and just glared at him. 'I—I'll contact the ambassador, or the consulate or the—the...' Her voice tailed off as she realized that she actually didn't have the first clue *whom* she should contact.

Zak al-Farisi surveyed her with maddening indifference, totally unmoved by her outburst. 'You have broken our laws and will stay here until your brother decides to show up and face me in person,' he responded, his tone dry and cynical as he stroked his fingers through the length of her tumbled blonde hair. 'In the meantime I feel sure that we will find a mutually agreeable way of relieving the boredom. Welcome to Kazban, Miss Kingston.'

CHAPTER TWO

Superb actress, Zak thought to himself, watching as Emily's cheeks paled and her deep blue eyes flew wide.

Suddenly she looked lost, scared and very, *very* young and had he not learned long ago to his cost just how convincingly women could act when they wanted something, he would have found himself taking her in his arms and reassuring her.

He gave a wry smile and reminded himself that she had travelled to Kazban in the place of her brother with the express intent of evading punishment for a serious crime. She was the sister of a criminal and he had no doubt that Emily Kingston wouldn't know innocent if she fell over it.

Doubtless her mode of dress and innocent approach were all part of her plan to persuade him to release her but he had no intention of doing anything of the sort. He would keep her here as a bargaining tool and Miss Kingston could use the time to dwell on the consequences of greed and avarice.

Did she not care that thousands of innocent citizens of Kazban had lost their entire savings?

She pleaded for two more months and yet she must have been fully aware that even two more years would not have been enough to see the debt repaid. How could it, when his investigations had shown clearly that her brother was on the verge of bankruptcy and involved in some *extremely* shady dealings?

And how could one so beautiful be so greedy and morally corrupt?

He stared at her face in fascination, captivated by her wide eyes and lush mouth and by the gentle flush that touched her cheeks. He felt muscles tighten throughout his body, felt the powerful flame of arousal kindle and burn, and gritted his teeth in irritation, forced to concede that the mixture of sexy and innocent was having a shockingly powerful effect on his libido. Even knowing what she was, it seemed he was unable to control his body's primitive response to her exceptional beauty and suddenly he found himself fighting a powerful impulse to strip her naked and spread her over his desk to await his pleasure.

For a brief moment black eyes clashed with blue and then he muttered something in Arabic and exercised the willpower for which he was renowned, stepping away from her and pacing once more towards the window. But that brief glance into her eyes had told him what he wanted to know.

That she was as aware of him as he was of her. The heavy throb of sexual awareness had hung in the air from the moment she'd stepped into the room and he recognized the same white-hot sexual excitement in her that he was experiencing himself.

But it made not an iota of difference to his plans.

Once before.

Once before he'd allowed his desire for a woman to overrule his common sense and he'd learned a painful lesson. He did *not* need to be taught that lesson twice.

Despite her pretence at innocence, he had no intention of releasing Emily Kingston until her brother arrived in person, no matter how much her lower lip trembled or how powerful his own arousal.

'You can't just keep me here against my will.' Her voice was strangled. 'What do you intend to do? Lock me in your tower?'

Despite the defiant lift of her chin her voice shook and Zak gave an amused smile. 'You have been reading too many fairy stories, Miss Kingston. This particular prince has a much more contemporary approach to incarceration.' His eyes swept her face. 'You'll find my bed much more hospitable than any tower and I promise that any form of bondage will only be with mutual consent.'

She gave a soft gasp of shock and Zak watched with interest as her breathing quickened and bright spots of colour appeared on her cheeks. She was obviously determined to keep up the innocent act to the last. He wondered idly whether she'd still be protesting innocence when she was stretched naked beneath him and decided to play her game for a little bit longer.

'Y-you can't be serious.' She stammered the words out, the confusion on her pretty face interesting to watch. 'I— you can't possibly want me to—I mean—'

'I can do anything I wish, Miss Kingston. You are in my country,' he pointed out calmly, 'and will remain so until your brother chooses to repay the debt.'

She shook her head and strands of that delicious blonde hair wafted around her heart-shaped face.

'This is ridiculous. You *have* to let me go—' There was a catch in her voice and Zak surveyed her with a mixture of admiration and amusement. He'd had endless experience of the application of feminine tears, but, even so, she was impressive. Her display was all the more effective for the fact that she didn't actually let the tears fall, he reflected. Instead she lifted her chin and struggled for control so that she managed to make herself look brave.

'Doubtless you were banking on that when you foolishly agreed to take your brother's place. When he arrives, you are free to leave,' he said shortly, turning away from her and striding over to the window, inexplicably irritated by the definite sparkle of tears in her eyes.

Women, he thought to himself, sucking in a breath as he fought to control the powerful and thoroughly unexpected reaction of his body to her award-winning performance.

'But all he asks is for two months more to sort things out,' she persisted. 'Is it really too much to ask? Does the money really matter that much?'

He whirled round, deeply offended by her implication that *he* was the one at fault and by her repeated dismissal of the debt. His temper rising steadily, he paced around her like a caged tiger, searching for some evidence of remorse on her part.

She was so close that he could count every one of those thick lashes that fringed her eyes, see the tiny pulse beating in her creamy throat, and he gave an exclamation of distaste as lust, basic and powerful, gnawed greedily at his body once more.

Beautiful on the outside maybe, but *not* on the inside.

'Your brother has committed a crime which is punishable by imprisonment here in Kazban.' His tone was harsh and he stopped pacing and took a step towards her. 'If he truly believed that by sending you in his place he could evade our justice system, then he made a serious error of judgment. I shall keep you here until he comes in person to face the charges against him.'

'C-crime?' Slim fingers pushed her blonde hair out of her startled eyes. 'The value of investments has fallen for everyone. That's just a risk you take, surely. It certainly isn't a *crime*.'

Zak watched her in incredulous disbelief, appalled by the fact that she was still pretending to know nothing about the fact that her brother had embezzled the money. How long could she keep that up? he wondered cynically. Peter Kingston had lost every last penny. He'd mortgaged the family home and was virtually bankrupt. How long could his sister continue to pursue the defence that the loss was attributable to the vagaries of the markets?

'My brother will pay you what he owes you,' she said firmly, her chin lifting as she looked at him. 'You can't keep me here.'

Her chest rose and fell as she breathed and a man less experienced with women than Zak might have missed the sudden parting of her soft lips or the press of her hardened nipples against the thin fabric of her dress as she stared at him in terrified fascination.

But with the razor-sharp intuition that had guaranteed him staggering success in both the boardroom and the bedroom, Zak didn't miss a single signal and he gave a grim smile of masculine satisfaction.

Having failed to secure her release, she was already thinking about being in his bed—

His eyes dropped to her mouth and sexual awareness throbbed between them. She might be corrupt but she was astonishingly beautiful. Zak gritted his teeth, battling against the powerful reaction of his body. Suddenly the bed option held considerable appeal.

'I will keep you as long as you are of use to me,' he returned smoothly, watching as her lovely face drained of colour.

'No! That wasn't what Peter intended.' Her tone was frantic. 'He'll be expecting me home—'

'And when you don't arrive, then presumably he'll follow you here.' Zak surveyed her through lowered lids, finding her passionate defence of her brother entirely distasteful. Clearly she supported her brother's dishonest dealings and was determined to pretend that nothing was wrong. 'Unless he is too much of a coward to face me in person.'

'My brother is not a coward.' Her blue eyes sparked with anger and spots of colour appeared on her pale cheeks.

Zak watched with interest, intrigued by the change in her and wrestling with a basic desire to increase the colour in her cheeks still further with physical activity. 'Tell me, Miss Kingston...' he kept his tone conversational '...why did you agree to come here?'

'Because Peter was too busy to come himself,' she said immediately and then blushed slightly. 'And because I thought it might be an adventure. But it didn't occur to either of us that you'd make me stay instead,' she said stiffly. 'After all, I'm no use to you whatsoever.'

Her pretence at indifference was laughable.

Zak gritted his teeth, irritated that he could still want her even knowing what she was. 'Prepare yourself for adventure, Miss Kingston,' he advised softly. 'Your brother has committed a crime and unless he arrives in person to stand trial, then you will face that trial in his place.'

'Trial?' Her face blanched. 'But I haven't done anything.'

'You have come as your brother's representative,' Zak pointed out smoothly, 'which makes you liable for his crimes. That is justice.'

'Justice?' She shook her head and then brushed aside the blonde hair that wafted over her face. 'It doesn't sound like justice to me! You keep calling it a crime but none of this is his fault. And you can't make me face trial. You—'

'I can do anything I please,' Zak interrupted her, suddenly fighting an impulse to power her back against his desk and seek immediate payment in kind. Irritated by the extraordinarily powerful attraction that he suddenly felt, he hardened his tone. 'This is Kazban, not England, and our laws are somewhat stricter than yours when it comes to theft.'

She lifted a hand to her throat as if she was suddenly finding it hard to breathe. 'I don't know what you're talking about. My brother hasn't stolen anything. Investments are always a risk. They can go down as well as up.'

Zak blinked, unaccustomed to being lectured by anyone on the subject of finance. He had a degree in economics and an MBA from a top American university, and since he'd been forced to take over responsibility for running the country as a result of his father's ill health the economy of Kazban had gone from strength to strength. There was very little anyone could teach him about investments. And very little anyone could teach him about risk.

He thrived on risk.

Did the Kingstons really expect him to believe that the loss was a result of changes in the stock market when he knew full well that the money had never been invested?

Deciding to play her game for a little longer, he kept his features impassive. 'Then you'd better pray they go up, Miss Kingston.' He surveyed her thoughtfully, wondering for how long she could maintain this pretence. 'And you'd better pray that your brother arrives here soon. Otherwise I advise you to prepare yourself for an extended stay.'

'But—'

'This audience is now at an end,' he said coldly. 'There are others waiting to see me. You will stay at the palace until your brother arrives. That is my decision.'

She had to get away.

She'd come here to help Peter, but her presence had made things worse.

The prince obviously intended to use her as leverage against her brother.

'You'll find my bed much more hospitable than any tower—'

Suddenly finding it hard to breathe, Emily grabbed her few possessions and stuffed them frantically into the one, small overnight bag that she'd brought with her. It was perfectly obvious that Crown Prince Zak al-Farisi wasn't going to listen to reason and release her, which meant that she needed to take matters into her own hands.

The man might *look* gorgeous, but he was ruthless and cold and not at *all* a nice person.

Why was he pressing her brother for the money when he was obviously rolling in it?

Just how much money did one man need?

Never having been in the slightest bit interested in material possessions, Emily struggled to understand why someone would strive for unlimited wealth.

Having lost both her parents when she was twelve, her own idea of riches was to have her own family. A man who loved her. Children.

She swallowed hard as she stuffed the rest of her clothes into the bag.

One day she would have that, she told herself firmly.

And it would be with a man who was kind and loving and—and *safe*.

Not a man like Zakour al-Farisi who was hard and unforgiving and obviously only thought about money.

Her hands stilled and suddenly her breathing quickened as she remembered the betraying throb of her body and the heat that she'd felt when he'd stood close to her. No one had ever made her feel like that before. In fact before today she hadn't known that such powerful emotions existed except in books.

The blatantly sexual intent in his cold, hard gaze had made her shivery and dizzy and—and—*shocked*.

No man had ever looked at her the way he did.

No man had ever made her feel so—so... She closed her eyes and slid a hand slowly up her body. *No man had ever made her feel so much like a woman.*

She lifted a hand and touched her face, remembering the cool brush of his fingers against her cheek and then her hair. *Remembering the race of her pulse and the melting of her limbs.*

He'd barely touched her and yet the burning heat in his dark eyes had been enough to have her swaying towards him in an instinctive feminine response to his powerful masculinity. But then Zak al-Farisi was a man so skilled in the seduction of women that someone as inexperienced as her would be child's play to him.

Emily gripped the bag tightly with slender fingers and tried to pull herself together.

That she could respond that way to someone that she didn't even *like* filled her with dismay and confusion.

She'd always thought that for her sex was something that would happen within the confines of a loving relationship.

Unlike some of her peers, she'd never seen the attraction of casual sexual encounters. Until now.

You want him, she mocked herself gently. Go on, admit it. Zak al-Farisi might not be a nice person but *you want him.* And the thought of being taken to his bed—

She closed her eyes and gave a moan of self-loathing.

No!

She had no intention of being anyone's virgin sacrifice!

That wasn't the sort of relationship she wanted. That was just sex, and she wasn't interested in anything so fragile, however exciting it might seem. She'd long ago decided that when she finally fell for a man their relationship would be based on mutual respect and friendship.

So why did her dream for the future suddenly seem so solid and boring?

She gave a little shiver. Zak al-Farisi might be astonishingly good-looking but his charms definitely ended there. He was totally *unreasonable,* accusing Peter of some sort of crime when she knew that her brother would never do anything illegal and the whole situation was just the result of a misunderstanding. It had to be.

And there was no way she was going to allow the prince to keep her here.

She pushed the last of her things into her bag and bit her lip.

No one was going to hold her against her will!

Pushing aside the uncomfortable thought that what she was actually escaping from was a part of herself that she hadn't known existed before today, she gritted her teeth, jerked the zip closed and tossed the bag on the floor.

The airport hadn't been that far away, she reasoned as she slipped her passport into the pocket of her dress. All she had to do was to persuade someone to give her a lift.

And leave the palace without getting caught—

She walked over to the windows of her room and stared thoughtfully down into the courtyard three floors below. Not far. Her eyes drifted to the elaborate curtains and then to the rope that held them back. Just like the ropes in the gym at school, she mused, fingering the rope thoughtfully.

Strong enough to take a person's weight.

It was fortunate that she was athletic.

'Miss Kingston has left the palace, Your Highness.'

Zak lifted his head. He was fresh from studying the expenses of his sister-in-law, and his patience was already severely challenged.

'How?'

Sharif cleared his throat. 'She—er—abseiled down the side of the building.'

Zak dropped the pen he was holding, his mind temporarily leaving the ever-absorbing question of how one woman could spend so much on so little. 'She *what*?'

Sharif licked his lips. 'She abseiled down the side of the palace, Your Highness. One of the guards saw her throw a rope out of the window but she moved so fast that he was unable to apprehend her.'

'A *rope*?' Zak thought back to their discussion about princes and being locked in his tower. 'Don't tell me,' he drawled. 'She spun the rope from her hair?'

Not party to the earlier conversation about fairy tales, Sharif looked confused. 'I understand that she used the cords from the curtains, Your Highness.'

'Of course she did.' Zak digested this information and then sat back in his chair and gave a reluctant laugh, stunned by the realization that he'd underestimated a woman for the first time in years. For sheer nerve and inventiveness you had to admire her, he conceded, rising to his feet and pacing across to the nearest window.

And if he'd needed further proof of her guilt, then he had it now.

Emily Kingston obviously didn't believe that there was any way her brother was going to turn up and rescue her.

But what had she hoped to achieve by escaping from the palace in such a way? Surely she knew that it was impossible for her to leave the country without his permission?

Did she really think that she could just shimmy down the palace wall and jump on a plane?

He gave Sharif a weary look, wondering why women had to be so complicated. 'You are having her followed?'

'Of course, Your Highness.'

'Good.' Zak gave a grim smile. 'Let her walk where she wishes and see where her escape bid takes her.'

Sharif looked startled. 'But, Your Highness, it isn't safe for her to be wandering the streets of Kazban. She—'

'Is in for a shock,' Zak finished for him, his dark eyes glittering with anticipation. 'I predict that a few hours alone in Kazban should make her desperate for my protection.'

The prospect afforded him a considerable degree of satisfaction.

Sharif looked troubled. 'But, Your Highness, for a woman as beautiful as Miss Kingston—' He licked his lips and broke off without finishing his sentence, suddenly remembering his place.

'This woman sanctions theft and corruption,' Zak reminded him curtly, rising to his feet in a lithe movement, his mouth set in a hard line. 'Let her see a little of the rougher side of Kazban.'

Perhaps it would teach her a lesson.

Sharif hesitated. 'But she was walking towards the *souk*, Your Highness, and the hour grows late. It will be dark shortly. It isn't safe for a western woman—'

'I agree with you entirely—' Zak's eyes glittered black '—but Emily Kingston is hardly an innocent virgin. She is obviously a woman well able to take care of herself. Let her see what can happen when she strays from the palace. In future she may not be quite so keen to leave it.'

Still looking troubled, Sharif bowed his head. 'There is one further problem that requires your urgent attention, Your

Highness.' His tone was apologetic. 'The nanny is finding it hard to cope with Jamal's tantrums.'

Zak closed his eyes briefly. 'Remind me.' His tone was weary. 'How long has she lasted, Sharif?'

Sharif cleared his throat. 'Four weeks, Your Highness. Longer than the last four. I'm sorry to burden you with the problem when you have so many other matters to attend to, but while your sister-in-law is still travelling—'

Gallivanting around Europe, leaving her child in the hands of someone who was clearly *not* up to the job, Zak reflected grimly. The knowledge that her presence in Kazban created more tension than any reasonable man could be expected to tolerate had made him reluctant to intervene and order her return home.

Concerns for his little nephew warred with his natural desire to minimize his own exposure to his sister-in-law's tricks.

Contemplating the facts with his customary cool, Zak decided that perhaps it really *was* time that he married. At least he could then put an end to Danielle's scheming in that direction.

'Surely there must be someone who can handle the child.' Zak sighed and leaned back in his chair. 'All right. I'll speak to Jamal.' He looked at Sharif expectantly and his eyes narrowed. 'There's more, isn't there?'

Sharif looked uncomfortable. 'It is now almost five years since your brother's tragic death, Your Highness. His widow is—' He broke off and licked dry lips. 'There have been pictures—your father is asking questions. He is afraid that there will be another scandal.' Sharif cleared his throat delicately. 'It is no secret that your father hopes that you will wed your brother's widow—'

Zak sat totally still, not a muscle flickered in his handsome face.

It was definitely time he married. And it wouldn't be to his sister-in-law.

Any woman would be preferable to her.

To think that he'd once—

His jaw tightened as he contemplated the foolishness of youth. Although he was now firmly of the belief that love did not exist, he was convinced that he could do better in his choice of bride than a woman who put her own needs ahead of those of her child.

He would *not* be marrying Danielle.

Zak gave a sigh, the prospect of marriage leaving him profoundly depressed. There were many occasions when the duty and responsibility accorded to his role felt like an unyielding block of concrete around his neck.

When he finally had his emotions back under control, he spoke. 'I will deal with my late brother's wife.'

With a wave of his hand he dismissed Sharif and lounged back in his chair, his dark eyes narrowed as he considered his next move.

Suddenly all he could think of was Emily Kingston.

He stared down at the pages of figures on his desk, but his mind was filled with disturbing images of honey-blonde hair and a soft, tempting mouth.

Doubtless she had done nothing to disguise that amazing blonde hair or those lush curves before making her bid for freedom. The knowledge that those charms were now on the streets of Kazban, visible to all, did nothing for his concentration.

With a rough exclamation he rose to his feet and stared at the sky, noting the deepening blue, acknowledging that Sharif was right. It would be dark in an hour. And Emily Kingston was alone.

Making an instant decision, he cursed softly and hit a series of buttons on his phone.

He'd sort out the problem with his nephew and his sister-in-law later. First he had to deal with Emily Kingston.

* * *

Unable to believe that she'd managed to leave the palace without being apprehended, Emily sneaked a glance over her shoulder, but there was no sign of anyone following her. Her heart was thudding and her palms were damp and she'd never felt such panic in her life before. She'd barely been able to breathe, choked with anticipation, expecting to feel a hand on her shoulder at any moment.

But there had been no hand. She'd done it.

Now all she had to do was find a car to take her to the airport.

Where on earth did one find a taxi in Kazban?

The initial panic fading, she was suddenly aware of just how hot it was away from the cool interior of the palace. Even though it was early evening, the sun hammered down on the dusty streets and the air was stifling.

Wishing that she had a hat and feeling more than a little vulnerable, she clutched her one small bag and walked as fast as she could in her one pair of ridiculous heels, trying to ignore the fact that she was boiling to death in her jacket. There was no way she was removing it. She had no wish to draw attention to herself and she knew that, although her dress fell to her ankles, it revealed far too much of her arms and shoulders to be considered decent in a country such as Kazban. So she gritted her teeth and kept the jacket on, promising herself that as soon as she was safely on the airplane she'd take it off and cool herself down.

She walked through the *souk*, wondering which direction to take, distracted by the colourful stalls and the wonderful smells.

Spices.

Intrigued, Emily paused by a stall heaped high with dune-like mountains of turmeric and many other spices that she didn't recognize. Next to the spice stall someone was cooking, the clatter of pans and the sizzle of hot fat cutting through the dry, still air, the smells delicious and tempting.

She wandered on, past stalls where men dressed in traditional robes sold brightly coloured silks, past boxes and boxes of exotic nuts and sweets, fruits and vegetables.

Once she tried asking about a taxi and the man waved his arms vaguely. She tried to follow his directions but there were just more and more stalls and no sign of anything that even remotely resembled a taxi.

The light was fading fast and she realized that she was lost in the middle of Kazban, with absolutely no idea where she was.

Feeling decidedly uneasy, she turned back the way she'd come and looked at the maze of dusty streets, trying to remember her route.

When exactly had the bustle and activity ceased? The streets were eerily quiet, as if she were the only person inhabiting this corner of the planet.

Wishing that someone else would appear, she started to walk down the nearest street and then stopped dead as three men dressed in robes suddenly blocked her path.

Her heart gave a jolt of panic.

One of them spoke to her in a language that she didn't understand and when she didn't answer they circled around her, blocking her escape.

Instinctively Emily clutched at her bag even though there was virtually nothing in it and her passport was safely tucked into a pocket in her dress.

The tallest of them spoke again and this time he smiled, but it was such an unpleasant, threatening smile that Emily felt a shiver of fear.

Determined not to give him the satisfaction of knowing that he'd frightened her, she lifted her chin boldly and tried to sidestep past the men, but they closed in more tightly, throwing remarks to each other that she didn't understand.

One of them reached out and grabbed a handful of her hair, twisting it around his fingers as though he were considering a purchase.

'Leave me alone!' Heart galloping like a horse's hooves,

Emily jerked her head away from his touch and took a step backwards, but one of his friends was directly behind her, blocking her escape.

She had nowhere to go.

CHAPTER THREE

SHE was in huge trouble.

Emily glanced frantically around her, searching for an alternative escape route. But there was none. And already the men were closing in. Before she could move, one of them made a grab for her bag and another dragged her jacket from her shoulders.

Suddenly she was standing in the dusty streets wearing nothing but her thin cotton dress and a pair of ridiculous shoes.

For a moment she stood still, breathing rapidly, frozen with fear. And then some of the fear melted away to be replaced by anger. She was a visitor to a foreign country. She should be treated with respect and courtesy.

'I'm English.' She spoke slowly and clearly. 'Give me my things back.'

They leered at her and, acting on a sudden impulse, she flew at the man who'd taken her bag, kicking him so hard with one of her shoes that he gave a yelp and doubled up in pain and surprise.

'Finally I understand the origin of the term "killer heels",' Emily muttered, snatching at her bag and making a run for it.

Her triumph was short-lived. Temporarily stunned by her surprise attack, the man's two comrades suddenly came to life and grabbed her bodily. Her dress tore, she lost the bag and crashed awkwardly to the ground, wincing as something cut into her ankle.

'Ouch—!' Gritting her teeth against the pain, she lifted her head, furious and ready to fight—and then she saw a fourth man striding towards them, his robes flowing back from his powerful frame.

He was taller and broader than the men who surrounded her and walked with a grim sense of purpose that made Emily shiver. His head was covered by the traditional *gutra* and she caught a glimpse of fierce black eyes before he strode forward and snapped something in a strange language, one bronzed hand resting ominously on the folds of his robes as he scanned the scene.

Friend or foe?

Emily held her breath, her eyes fixed on his hand. She knew instinctively that the folds of his robes concealed a weapon. Would there be a fight? But those long, strong fingers stayed still as his eyes flickered slowly over her attackers.

One by one they fell back, at first resentful and then visibly intimidated by the menace in that dark gaze and the physical power and authority that pulsed from his masculine frame.

And then they turned and ran, taking Emily's bag and jacket with them.

Emily clutched the torn neck of her dress and started to shake, her eyes fixed on the man who had caused their flight.

Without uttering a word, her rescuer bent down and scooped her into his arms.

'What are you doing?' Taken by surprise, Emily thumped his shoulder with her fist and made contact with rock solid muscle. 'Put me down!'

'Be still!' He tightened his grip on her, carrying her as if she weighed nothing, striding purposefully through a network of narrow, dusty streets until he finally came to a halt in a secluded doorway.

'Are you hurt?' He snapped the question in perfect English and to her horror Emily felt the mortifying burn of tears.

It was just the shock, she told herself, struggling to restrain the impulse to sob against his broad shoulder. Now that she was safe she suddenly realized just how close she'd been to real danger. *If he hadn't arrived when he had—*

'I'm fine,' she lied, glancing around her dubiously. 'You can put me down. Why have you brought me here? It looks more dangerous than the main street—'

'You were drawing too much attention to yourself,' the man said harshly, but he lowered her to the ground with surprising gentleness, muttering something under his breath as he glanced down.

'You are bleeding.'

Emily followed his frowning gaze and suddenly realized why her leg was hurting so badly. Blood was pouring from a deep cut on her ankle.

'Oh—I must have cut it on something when I was attacked.'

'Which would not have happened had you not been walking in an unsafe area.' He gave a sigh that spoke volumes and then squatted down so that he could take a closer look. In an impatient gesture he moved her skirt and slid strong fingers over her ankle. 'No wonder you are injured,' he growled. 'These shoes are ridiculous.'

'I totally agree, but they're the only pair I brought with me,' Emily protested, wincing as he slid the shoe off and examined her bruised ankle. 'I wasn't exactly planning on having to run for my life when I packed. Ouch, you're hurting me!'

'You should be thankful that it is only your ankle that is hurt,' he said, his tone blisteringly unsympathetic as he finished his examination. 'I don't think it will need stitches. Next time you try to escape I suggest you select your footwear more carefully.'

Emily's eyes widened and she looked at him closely for the first time. 'How did you know that I was escaping—?'

With a jerk of his hand he removed something from his neck and bandaged her foot deftly, stemming the flow of blood. Then he lifted his gaze to hers and she fell into those fierce dark eyes. The breath jammed in her throat as she recognized him.

'Oh—no—*it's you*!'

He inclined his proud head, his mouth set in a hard line as he surveyed her. 'Indeed. I trust my mode of dress meets with your satisfaction on this occasion, Miss Kingston.'

Staring up at him, Emily lost her ability to breathe normally. She'd thought he looked good in a suit, but it was nothing compared to his appearance in the traditional robes of his countrymen. How could she have failed to recognize him?

Even in the dusky light he was extravagantly handsome and he held himself with an arrogance that spoke of centuries of breeding.

No wonder the other men had run—

'Clearly I should have locked you in my tower after all,' he observed in a chilly tone, rising to his feet in a fluid movement and glancing left and right down the narrow street. 'It would have been safer for everyone. You could do with forgetting your fairy stories while you are in Kazban, Miss Kingston. This particular prince is not about to play his part according to the book. If you're expecting Prince Charming, then you are doomed to disappointment.'

'I never went a bundle on Prince Charming,' Emily confessed shakily, her eyes still stuck to his face, watching hopefully to see if there was some softening of his attitude towards her now that he knew that she was serious about escaping. There didn't seem to be. He was grim-faced and furiously angry.

'Then let's take a look at reality. A large number of people have been put to a great deal of trouble on your behalf,' he bit out, his dark eyes glittering with impatience as he stared down at her. 'My presence was required in the palace this evening but because of your foolhardy activities I have been forced to risk giving offence to those whose good relations are essential for maintaining peace in this area.'

Emily looked up at him guiltily. 'I didn't ask anyone to follow me,' she began, and Zak al-Farisi threw back his handsome head and muttered something incomprehensible under his breath. She didn't need a translation to know that his words hadn't been flattering.

'Had we not followed you, Miss Kingston, you would now be at the mercy of those men who were showing such an interest in you when I arrived. The palace guards lost you for a moment and have been combing the streets for the last two hours and everywhere they went there was talk of a beautiful Western woman with hair like crushed silk.' His mouth hardened and his black gaze mocked her. 'Certain areas of Kazban are not safe for a Western woman to walk alone. From now on you would find it safer to remain at the palace. Step outside and there are any number of risks. The heat, the desert, hostile tribes—'

A drop-dead gorgeous prince...

Emily stared up at him, heart pounding, thinking that she was probably looking at the biggest risk of them all.

Him.

Feeling thoroughly confused and unsettled, she winced as pain shot through her ankle. 'I just wanted to go home.'

He gazed at her with undiluted exasperation. 'And how far did you think you'd get, dressed like that?'

She glanced down at herself and then gasped in horror as she realized that the torn neck of her dress was gaping, exposing an indecent amount of creamy flesh. Blushing furiously, she jerked the edges of her dress together and glared at him. 'I was wearing a jacket until they stole it,' she pointed out, 'along with my bag.'

'And all that golden hair was streaming down your back in a blatant invitation,' he bit out impatiently and she sucked in a breath, indignation making her indifferent to protocol.

'Well, that's your fault! You dragged the clip out in the

palace and I lost it,' she croaked, wondering why there suddenly seemed to be no oxygen in the air. She was breathing in and out but her head was starting to swim. Telling herself that it had nothing to do with the fact that he was standing so close to her, she straightened up, her expression frosty. 'And for your information, I looked for a hat in the *souk* but I couldn't find one.'

'Hats are for tourists and you were in the wrong part of the *souk* for such a purchase.' He made an impatient gesture and then stiffened as they both heard shouts coming from nearby.

Emily gave a gasp of dismay and immediately he covered her mouth with the flat of his hand, plastering her back into the doorway with the force of his body, concealing her from view.

'Quiet!' His soft command made her aware of just how foolish she'd been to think she could find her own way through this unfamiliar city. If he hadn't found her—

Emily closed her eyes and the shouts faded into the background. Suddenly all she was aware of was the pulsing heat of the late-evening sun and the hard muscle of his powerful thighs pressed against hers. She felt the strength of his body protecting hers, heard the harshness of his breathing as he concealed her with the folds of his robes. Lost in a world that she'd never entered before, she breathed in his tantalizing male scent and let the force and strength of his body wrap around her. A strange weakness spread through her limbs and her lips parted under the firm pressure of his hand. Suddenly the urge to taste him was overpowering and her tongue flickered over lean, bronzed fingers.

She heard his sharp intake of breath, heard him mutter something under his breath and then his hand shifted. Without warning, his fingers slid roughly into the silken mass of hair that tumbled over her shoulders, tilting her head, exposing her to the full impact of his savage black gaze.

She heard the ragged intake of his breath, saw anger and fire in his eyes and then his mouth came down on hers with punishing force, stifling her cry of shock with the heat of his kiss.

Excitement cascaded through her body and she melted against him, seduced by the erotic slide of his tongue in her mouth, the throb of his body pressed intimately against hers. She felt the warmth and strength of his hand as it moved down her spine and then she was hauled hard against him, the softness of her body merging with the hardness of his.

Drowning in sensation, Emily tried to struggle to the surface but the shocking press of his arousal and the lick of his tongue sent her spiralling out of control, dizzy and weak with an excitement so intense and unfamiliar that she didn't know how to fight it. It was impossible to know where she ended and he began, their bodies locked together in a sensual combat so powerful that both seemed unable to halt the madness.

Another shout penetrated the fog of white-hot sexual desire, cutting through frenzied passion as effectively as the sharpest sword through the finest silk. Suddenly his mouth lifted from hers and she staggered slightly as he stepped away from her, his bronzed, handsome face set in an expression so grim that she stared at him in bemusement, her body still howling protest at the cessation of such delicious and previously undiscovered pleasures.

She ached all over. *Ached for him to finish what he'd started.*

And yet at the same time she was utterly horrified at her inability to control her response to him. *She shouldn't have felt that way.* It made absolutely no sense. How was it possible to dislike a person and yet want to cling to him and learn every part of his body?

She should have slapped his face. She should have pushed him away. The fact that *he'd* been the one to end the contact left her shrinking with mortification. 'That should *not* have happened,' he ground out, taking another step backwards, as if not trusting himself to stand within touching distance. 'In Kazban we do not indulge in such public displays.'

Emily stared at him, mute, wondering which one of them was most shocked.

Him, by displaying what accounted for a serious lapse in his legendary self-control, or her, by discovering that such a level of sexual excitement even existed. She'd always thought that the pleasures of sex were grossly exaggerated. Had never had any reason to think otherwise. Certainly the few kisses she'd indulged in since she'd reached adolescence had induced nothing but boredom. She'd assumed that perhaps she wasn't a very sexual person.

But now she knew differently and the fact that it was this man who had made her discover that fact just *appalled* her.

Had she no taste?

'We should leave,' he said grimly, 'before the situation deteriorates further.'

Which situation? Emily stared dizzily into his proud, arrogant face, wondering whether he was talking about the risk from the locals or the risk from her.

Clearly he was less than impressed by the kiss. But then the guy had a troop of women willing to amuse him, she thought wistfully. One kiss with her in a dark alleyway was hardly going to fire his blood, was it?

'Where are your security guards?'

His dark gaze was enigmatic. 'Nearby, should I require them. But I don't. I am more than able to defend myself should the need arise. Which is more than can be said for you.'

She rallied slightly at his tone. 'I could have rescued myself if I'd had to.'

'With what?' His voice was harsh and threaded with contempt and anger. 'Apart from causing severe injury with the heels of your shoes, what other weapons are contained in that one small bag? Exploding lip gloss? A poisoned hairbrush?'

Emily glared back, her eyes sparking. 'Stop mocking me.'

'I'm trying to make you see the risks involved in wandering around the streets of Kazban unaccompanied. Those men were not playing games. And now we must leave.'

He lifted his fingers to his mouth and gave a low whistle. Emily heard the thunder of hooves and then gasped in astonishment as a black horse careered wildly towards them and shuddered to a halt next to Zak al-Farisi, snorting and tossing his handsome head as he stamped his hooves impatiently.

Emily caught her breath at the beauty of the animal.

Horses were her abiding love and with two of her own at home she could more than appreciate the value of the horse standing in front of her.

She gave a half-smile. In a way the animal reminded her of its master. Both were strong and powerful and decidedly dangerous.

Zak lifted a hand to the horse's bridle and spoke softly to the stallion and then jerked his head to Emily.

'Quickly.'

Realising that he was intending to take her back to the palace, she backed into the doorway and shook her head.

'I'm not going with you! I'm not—oh—' Before she could finish her protest, the prince had swung her onto the horse's back as if she weighed nothing and vaulted on behind her, his hands clasping the reins lightly as he urged the stallion forward through the rapidly darkening streets.

Despite all her experience with horses she'd never been on such a wild ride, never known such speed and strength in an animal. With rippling muscles and a fiery flash of his eyes the stallion pulled on his bridle, fretting to be given his head as he galloped through the dusty streets.

But the prince was the one in control. He held the horse slightly in check, controlling the pace to suit him, using skill to contain the horse's great strength and power. Man and horse at one.

At any other time Emily would have been awed by this spectacular display of horsemanship but all she could think was that she was being taken back to the palace, and that she was unlikely to be given the opportunity to escape again.

They swerved through a network of narrow streets and Emily clutched a handful of the horse's mane, praying that no one would walk into their path. She felt the strength of Zak's arm as he clamped her against him, felt the heat and hardness of his thighs pressing against hers as he propelled the horse forwards towards the safety of the palace.

She felt the ripple of muscle under her legs as the horse lengthened his stride, covering the ground with a speed that was nothing short of exhilarating.

Emily had expected to approach the Golden Palace from the magnificent front entrance, but instead the prince urged the horse around the walls that circuited the opulent building and finally turned down a narrow passageway. Guards saluted and fell back as they galloped past at a ridiculous pace and it occurred to Emily that everyone clearly recognized the prince, despite the fact that he'd been dressed like every other man in the *souk*.

Even inside the safety of the palace Zak didn't reduce the speed and Emily closed her eyes briefly as they thundered down the narrow passageway and then slithered to a dusty halt in an enormous courtyard.

An army of servants sprang forward and Zak dismounted with athletic grace and then turned to lift Emily off the powerful stallion. Immediately her ankle gave way and with a soft curse Zak scooped her into his arms and barked something in a language that she didn't understand. Several servants scurried off in the direction of the palace and Emily felt her face burn under the scrutiny of those who remained.

'You don't have to carry me,' she muttered and he lifted a dark eyebrow in her direction.

'You would prefer to lie in a heap in the courtyard for the rest of your stay?' His tone was dry. 'You are already the subject of considerable speculation among my people. It would be wise not to give them additional fodder for gossip.'

Emily chewed her lip. 'I don't want to stay at all—I want to go home.'

'And that is not something for public discussion.' He carried her across the courtyard, seemingly oblivious to the banks of staff who positively flattened themselves as he approached.

Zak strode down acres of marbled corridor until he finally reached the room she'd been in that morning and, without saying a word, he deposited her with surprising gentleness on the silk couch, among a pile of soft cushions.

'A doctor will be with you shortly.'

She struggled to sit up. 'A doctor?'

He glanced at her impatiently. 'In case you have forgotten, your ill-conceived escape plan caused damage to your ankle. In the circumstances, you are fortunate that your injuries were so slight and that you are safe.'

Shivering with the memory of what might have happened, Emily closed her eyes briefly. 'Well, for your information, I don't exactly feel safe with you either. Why do you think I tried to escape in the first place?'

'Then your instincts are more reliable than I gave you credit for,' he drawled, his eyes glittering with an emotion that she couldn't interpret. 'I am most definitely not safe, Miss Kingston, but given the choice I think you might find my arms considerably warmer than the alternative. You should have planned your trip with more care,' he returned, his features set in aggressive lines. 'There was never even the slightest chance that you would be allowed to leave. Both you and your brother must have known that.'

'Of course he didn't know that! Peter would never send me into danger,' she said hotly and his mouth curved into a mocking smile.

'And yet you are here, Miss Kingston.'

She sucked in more air. 'Well, neither of us knew what a *totally* unreasonable, ruthless, suspicious—' She broke off and swallowed with horror as she remembered just whom she was speaking to '—er—Your Highness.'

'Please.' He spread bronzed hands in mocking invitation, his dark gaze sardonic as he surveyed her. 'I think we have long moved beyond the realms of palace protocol.'

She lifted her chin. 'I'm sorry, it's just that you—you make me angry. I suppose now you're going to clap me in irons and throw me in the dungeon.'

'You are obsessed with towers and dungeons.' With an impatient glance in her direction he paced over to the window and stared down into the courtyard. 'If I had any sense then that is exactly what I would do with you,' he muttered and Emily glared at him, stung by the injustice of his remark.

'Well, maybe you should if I'm such a dangerous criminal.'

There was a long, pulsing silence and then he turned his head and their eyes clashed, the memory of that kiss throbbing between them.

Zak al-Farisi strode towards her and lifted her to her feet, brushing aside silken blonde hair from her burning face with a strong hand, his handsome face grim.

'Do not provoke me, Miss Kingston,' he warned softly, his eyes fierce as he stared down at her. 'You are a walking temptation even for the most self-disciplined of men, and my needs are no less for knowing what you are.'

His mouth hovered above hers and Emily felt her heart bang against her ribs.

His features were strong and masculine, his jaw blue-black with stubble and his shoulders broad and powerful. It was no wonder the three men who'd attacked her had run, she thought weakly. He was more of a man than any man she'd ever met and she had an almost overwhelming urge to grab his robes and kiss him again.

Shocked by her own thoughts and feelings, Emily lifted a shaking hand to her throat.

She was going mad. This man was as harsh as the desert landscape she'd passed on her way to Kazban. He was her enemy. And she certainly didn't want to kiss him again.

The last occasion had left her in a state of shock.

And perhaps he was thinking the same thing because he made an impatient sound and turned away from her, unbuckling something from the folds of his cloak and laying a sword on the desk in front of him.

Emily's gaze followed his movements. 'So you do carry a weapon—'

'Be thankful that I did not have cause to use it,' he said harshly, turning back to face her. 'I would not have you add bloodshed to your list of crimes.'

'That's the second time you've mentioned crime and I haven't done anything.' Her eyes blazed into his. 'I have never committed crime of any sort in my life.' She stumbled over the words in her furious attempt to defend herself. 'I am *totally* honest and if you're such a lousy judge of character that you can't see that then I feel sorry for you—' She broke off, frozen into horrified stillness by the shock she saw in those dark eyes.

She bit back a groan of remorse. She just didn't recognize herself around this man! Normally she was easygoing and patient—she dealt with a class of twenty-six five year olds and *never* raised her voice and here she was suddenly being so rude that she was shocking herself.

And she was obviously shocking him too, if the incredulous expression on his proud features was anything to go by.

She held her breath, bracing herself for the comeback, but then his hard mouth curved into a cynical smile.

'Actually I'm an exceptionally good judge of character,

Miss Kingston,' he said dryly. 'Extreme wealth demands the development of such skills at a remarkably early age.'

She looked at him, her heart beating wildly. She didn't know about the rest of her sex, but when she looked at him she certainly wasn't thinking about money.

'I don't know anything about the other women who have crossed your path,' she stammered angrily, 'but I refuse to let you judge me by their standards.'

His gaze was sardonic. 'You, of course, have no interest in money.'

'No, I don't, actually.' She was goaded by the mockery in his tone. 'If you ask me, money causes nothing but problems! If there's one thing I've learned in life it's that money isn't important at all. Money can't buy you the things that *really* matter—' She broke off, breathless, suddenly aware of the tension in his powerful frame.

He leaned against his desk and looked at her, thick, dark lashes shielding his expression. 'And what is it that *really* matters to you, Miss Kingston?'

Something in that glittering black gaze made her heart thump against her chest. 'I can't believe you're in the slightest bit interested in what matters to me.'

'Tell me.' It was a command that couldn't be ignored and she swallowed hard, her eyes sliding away from his.

'Love,' she croaked helplessly, tumbling headlong into his exotic dark eyes, 'and family. You can't buy those things and they're worth more than all the money in the world. I want to meet a man who I can love and who loves me back. I want a home and children. That's all I want, Your Highness. That's all I've ever wanted.'

There was a long, pulsing silence and then his hard mouth curved into a smile.

'So you really do live in fairy-tale land. Love?' His eyes mocked her. 'You sound like an innocent child and we both know you're far from that.' As if to illustrate his point, his gaze dropped to the curve of her breasts, freely displayed by the torn material of her dress.

Her cheeks flooded with colour under the burning heat of his masculine gaze and suddenly she could hardly breathe. She struggled to her feet and made for the door, gritting her teeth as white hot pain shot through her ankle, not caring where she was going but just determined to get away from him. 'I don't care what you say, I'm *not* staying here. I'm going home.'

CHAPTER FOUR

STRONG fingers closed around Emily's wrist, halting her escape.

Zak al-Farisi stared down at her, fabulous dark eyes glittering with intent. 'You don't want me to let you go, Emily.' His voice was the soft purr of a lethal predator. 'I know exactly what you want, and it isn't that.'

He lifted a hand and slid long fingers into the revealing gap in her dress. With agonizing slowness and punishing intimacy, he dragged a finger over her hardening nipple and she cried out as sensation stabbed through her. Stunned and shocked by the violence of her own response to him, she heard his low laugh of masculine triumph through a haze of pleasure.

'You don't want me to let you go, do you, Emily?' His voice was slightly thickened and he powered her back against the door that had been her hope of escape, holding her there, locked against him. 'And don't try denying what you feel. The chemistry was strong between us from the moment you walked into my palace.'

'No!' But her shocked denial was meaningless because her body was pressing against his and she was having trouble thinking, let alone speaking. Once again her body was consumed by a burning need so powerful that it took her breath away.

She wanted him.

She wanted him so badly that she could hardly breathe and even though she *hated* herself for feeling that way, she couldn't stop herself.

She lifted a hand to push him away but her fingers felt the hard musculature of his broad chest and what had begun as self-protection turned swiftly to a sensual exploration. Her traitorous fingers slid up to his shoulders and down his arms, feeling the swell of muscle and the strength in his powerful frame.

She stared up at him dizzily, trying to remind herself that Zak al-Farisi was ruthless and hard-hearted and had shown her not one shred of kindness since she'd arrived in his country.

But her brain was refusing to work. Her body was dominated by sensation and she felt the intense ache of excitement increase as she breathed in his masculine scent, felt the press of his hard thighs against her.

'Still pretending that you want me to let you go, Emily?' His voice was a dark, husky drawl that teased her nerve endings and her insides tumbled with a sexual desire so intense that she gave a little moan.

'What are you doing?'

'Exactly what you intended me to do from the moment you turned up instead of your brother.' His mouth hovered tantalizingly close to hers. 'I'm taking that which was freely offered at a time when I am able to take full advantage of such a prize. You offered it in the *souk* but you need to learn that as a people we prefer such intimate encounters to take place behind closed doors.'

He thought that the kiss in the *souk* had been *her* fault? And yet it had been *his* hand that had covered her mouth, *his* hand that had asked to be tasted and touched.

'You've definitely read the wrong script,' she mumbled, just *hating* herself for being unable to control her body's reaction to him. 'The prince is supposed to kiss the princess and then release her, not imprison her—'

His mouth came down on hers with decisive force, his body hard against hers, holding her captive. Emily gave a gasp of shock, which turned to a whimper of need as his strong hands slid into her hair, anchoring her head as his mouth plundered hers.

She felt the erotic probe of his tongue against her mouth and her lips parted in response to his explicit demand. And she was lost. An ocean of sensation crashed over her, drowning thought and speech with its frightening intensity.

Transported by the heat of his mouth and the intimate stroke of his tongue, Emily tumbled into another world. A world she didn't recognize. A world where sensation ruled and where there were no rules. Just instinct. She felt the heat of his body against the throb of her heart and her whole body quivered and then melted.

He was all hard muscle and rampant masculinity and her fingers explored the width of his shoulders as she arched against him, the pain in her ankle temporarily forgotten as she tried to draw closer to him.

Desire coiled in her stomach, intensifying with each second until she was in an agony of sexual excitement, consumed by a fever that she'd never experienced before.

When he suddenly dragged his mouth away from hers she swayed towards him again, her whole body a trembling mass of sensation. She felt sick with disappointment that he'd stopped and even sicker with herself for wanting a man who fell so far short of her ideals.

It infuriated her that, despite everything she knew about him, it took only one touch of his clever mouth and she was willing to fall at his feet and declare undying allegiance.

Realising just how uninhibited she'd been, Emily stared at the ground, totally mortified. She'd virtually crawled all over him and if he hadn't stopped when he had she would have done *anything*—

How had that happened?

How had he managed to make her forget everything once again? *Like the fact that he was holding her prisoner.*

She tried to speak but no sound came out and she decided that she just didn't know her body around this man. It just didn't seem to function in the usual way. She looked up at him, misty-eyed, her brain foggy from the skill of his kiss, and finally managed to produce sound.

'I think maybe I do need that doctor after all.'

Zak strode down the lengthy corridors that led to his father's quarters, his body aching with unfulfilled sexual desire so intense that he contemplated stripping off his clothes and finding the nearest available cold fountain with which to cool his blood.

He gritted his teeth and muttered under his breath, oblivious to the staff who bowed deeply as he passed.

What was the matter with him?

He'd known that the girl was trouble from the moment she'd walked into his office, her huge eyes fixed on his face, and still he'd been overtaken by the most basic, primitive sexual urge that he'd ever experienced.

The mixture of innocence and passion had proved extraordinarily powerful and he, Zakour al-Farisi, who prided himself on his self-control above all else, had lost control. For a short time in the *souk* he'd forgotten everything except the softness of the woman trembling in his arms and the heat of her flesh burning against his. Had it not been for the shouts close by, he would have found himself jerking up her dress and taking her then and there, staking his claim to her in the doorway of a dusty street in the city he'd known and loved since he was a child.

He didn't know which was worse. The fact that he wanted her despite knowing what she was, or the fact that such a woman had driven him to a display so public that his face burned at the memory.

If anyone had seen them—

He reached his father's rooms and the guards fell back to allow him entry, their eyes flickering nervously to his grim, angry expression.

The proof that he was still as susceptible to an extremely

beautiful woman as the next man was doing nothing for the prince's temper.

It was just a physical attraction, he assured himself as he paced the last few steps to his father's private sitting room.

Despite her wide blue eyes and her injured air of innocence, Emily Kingston was no trembling virgin. It had been *her* tongue that had flickered temptingly over his fingers when he'd tried to silence her cry of alarm, *her* eyes that had begged him to act on the searing attraction that gripped both of them.

So why should he not take that which she was so freely offering?

It changed nothing.

He still intended to hold her brother to account for his crimes. His judgment in matters of business was still crystal clear. However powerful his feelings for Emily Kingston, they did not extend beyond the physical and they never would.

Having rationalized the situation to his satisfaction, Zak dismissed the guards and prepared to discuss serious matters of state with his father.

'You need to rest that ankle, Miss Kingston.'

'Ankle?' Emily stared at the elderly doctor blankly. She was back on the couch upholstered in gold silk and she wasn't even thinking about her ankle. She was just *seething* at the extraordinary arrogance of Zak al-Farisi.

He'd actually had the nerve to imply that she'd been determined to seduce him from the first, when *he'd* been the one who'd insisted on keeping her in his wretched palace! Given the chance she would have been on the first plane home!

And how she wished that had happened.

Emily gave a low groan and closed her eyes to the extreme consternation of the palace doctor.

But even closing her eyes didn't wipe out the memory of

his mouth on hers. Every nerve ending tingled and her body burned with an electrifying sensation that she didn't recognize.

'Miss Kingston?' the doctor prompted her urgently, a frown touching his wrinkled brow. 'Your pulse rate is very fast and your cheeks are flushed. Are you feeling all right?'

No! She felt terrible. And the next time she laid eyes on Zak al-Farisi he'd better be carrying his sword because she was so angry he was going to need to defend himself!

This was a man who had shown no gentleness towards her and who was accusing her brother of all sorts of unpleasant crimes. And now he seemed to think that she was some sort of seductress, just desperate for him to take her to bed!

Well, other women might be prepared to pander to his massive ego, but she had absolutely no intentions of increasing its already mammoth proportions!

Just because he knew how to kiss a woman senseless did *not* mean that she was going to lose sight of what sort of man he was.

The doctor lifted a hand to her forehead, looking more perplexed with each passing minute. 'You seem very agitated, Miss Kingston. Are you sure you didn't bang your head when you fell?'

'I'm fine,' she muttered stiffly and the doctor looked at her doubtfully.

'For the time being, you shouldn't do too much walking or the ankle could bleed again.' He gave her a hesitant smile and handed her a small bottle of tablets. 'I will leave you these painkillers and suggest that you sleep.'

Sleep?

Emily didn't think she'd ever sleep again! Every time she closed her eyes she fell into a vivid memory of fierce black eyes and a body that seemed to drive hers to a point of self-destruction.

She waited until the doctor had left the room and then breathed a sigh of relief. *Finally* she was alone.

She hobbled over to the desk and picked up the phone. She really needed to call her brother. One way or another, she *had* to get out of here and if that meant pleading with Peter to come, then that was what she'd do. Surely her brother would never have let her come had he known what the Crown Prince was really like?

'Calling the cavalry, Miss Kingston?'

His smooth tone came from the doorway and she dropped the phone guiltily and then reminded herself that this man expected women to lie down for him when he snapped his fingers and she wasn't going to do that.

If he thought that she was trying to seduce him, then he was in for a shock.

Her delicate chin lifted and she turned to face him. Immediately she wished she hadn't. It was much easier being angry with him when he was out of the room. When he was *in* the room all she could think of was—*was*—

'I was calling my brother,' she said stiffly. 'It seems clear to me that if you intend to keep me here until he arrives, then the sooner he arrives, the better. I have no desire to spend a moment longer in your company than is absolutely necessary.'

Apparently undisturbed by her frosty announcement, the prince closed the door behind him and strolled into the room with indolent grace, his expression unreadable. 'Please—' he extended a hand in a gesture of invitation, a flicker of amusement visible in his dark gaze '—feel free to make the call. I would also like to know what your brother has planned. If he has no intention of coming to your rescue then I will have to consider your future.'

Her heart took off like a racehorse with the finish line in sight. 'My future?'

He shrugged, infuriatingly calm. 'If you are staying in the palace then I'll need to find a use for you.'

Emily felt her body go liquid, all the fight draining out of her. 'If you're suggesting what I think you're suggesting—' She could barely breathe and he lifted a dark eyebrow.

'And what is it that you think I'm suggesting?'

She could feel her skin burning under the intensity of his fierce gaze and she curled her fingers into her palms. 'That you—that I—join your harem, or something—'

'My *harem*?' For a moment she saw incredulity flicker in those dark eyes and something that could have been amusement, but then it was gone and he was regarding her steadily, totally in command of the situation, arrogantly sure of himself.

Emily closed her eyes briefly, ready to fall through the floor with embarrassment and discomfort. 'Well, even if you don't actually have a harem,' she muttered, 'I'm sure you have a string of women absolutely desperate to satisfy your every whim and I ought to warn you that I'd be hopeless at that.'

'Hopeless at satisfying my every whim?'

'Hopeless at everything.' She licked dry lips. 'I'm not harem material—'

But even as she said the words her eyes dropped to his lips, fixing on the perfect curve of his hard mouth. All she could think about was the burn of his mouth against hers and suddenly her breasts felt heavy and she felt her nipples peak under the thin fabric of her dress.

'You will doubtless be relieved to hear that I am very broad-minded about who I admit to my harem,' he murmured softly, and she dragged her eyes away from his mouth and glared at him, furious by her own response to him and convinced that he was laughing at her.

But there was no trace of amusement in those heavy lidded dark eyes. Just brooding tension and searing masculine appraisal.

Emily cleared her throat nervously, trying to remind herself that she should be slapping his face. So why did her limbs feel so heavy? Why was her whole body throbbing with a need that she'd never felt before? 'I'm really not interested in your harem. I'm going to call my brother now.' Her heart was thudding madly and he gave a smile.

'Do that. I think we both know that he won't be there, but we'll continue this pretence a little longer. I'm actually finding that I can enjoy your innocent act. It's amazingly convincing.'

'Well, of course it's convincing,' she mumbled, casting him a sideways look. 'You seem to think that I'm some closet sex kitten but I can assure you that nothing could be further from the truth—'

'I'm sure you're the very embodiment of innocence, Miss Kingston.' His dark drawl was loaded with cynicism and Emily looked at him in dismay, realizing that he didn't believe her.

He really *did* think she was some sort of seductress.

She didn't know whether to be flattered or appalled, but she did know that it was time she went home before she did something that she'd seriously regret.

With a shaking hand she reached for the phone, wondering what Peter would say when she told him that the prince had no intention of releasing her until he arrived in person.

Would he come?

Remembering how firmly her brother had told her that he couldn't possibly attend the meeting in Kazban himself, Emily felt suddenly nervous.

She paused with her hand on the receiver and the prince lifted a dark eyebrow in silent mockery.

'Is something wrong?' His tone was infuriatingly smooth. 'Perhaps you are reluctant to call your brother in the presence of an audience because it will make it difficult to agree on your next course of action.'

Emily's eyes sparked in defence of her brother, and she lifted the receiver defiantly. She was going to speak to Peter, she vowed, stabbing the buttons angrily. And Crown Prince Zakour al-Farisi could learn the art of apology.

But her heart was thumping and her hand started to shake as she clutched the receiver to her ear.

What if Peter refused to come?

Part of her was only too aware that it had been Peter's inability to come to Kazban that had required her attendance in the first place.

She held the phone to her ear, letting it ring and ring, feeling the prince's gaze on her as she waited for an answer.

Deciding that her brother must still be at his office, she started again and dialled the office number. Finally she got through to her brother's secretary but their brief conversation left her even more troubled.

'I don't understand it.' A ripple of panic spread through her. Feeling suddenly out of her depth, Emily replaced the phone and rubbed a hand over her face. *Where was Peter?* 'His secretary says that he's phoned in to say that he's taking three weeks off and he hasn't left a contact number.'

But why would Peter take three weeks off without telling her? Without first checking that she was safely back from Kazban?

'How convenient. Suspicion is a natural consequence of great wealth and influence. You would do well to remember that, Miss Kingston. I don't take anyone at face value and I never get taken for a ride.' His mouth curved into a mocking smile.

Already worried sick about her brother, she didn't laugh. 'What are you implying?' She turned to face him, her eyes sparking with challenge. 'If you think that my brother would run from his responsibilities, then you're wrong. Peter has never run from anything in his life. H-he must have decided to take a holiday or something.'

But even to her ears it sounded unlikely. Why would her brother choose to take a holiday when his business was obviously in trouble?

And why would he not have mentioned it to her?

Something was very wrong.

She nibbled her lip anxiously, her overactive, tired mind running through all sorts of unpleasant scenarios.

Had something happened to her sister-in-law, Paloma?

Or to Peter himself?

But if that was the case then wouldn't someone just have called her? After all, Peter knew where she was.

Suddenly she felt lost and totally out of her depth.

Peter was the only family she had in the world and if he was in trouble then she really had to help him.

She *had* to get home.

Close to tears and racked with worry, she looked at the prince, the fight draining out of her. 'This is something to do with the money he owes you, isn't it?'

Black eyes held hers unflinchingly. 'You tell me, Miss Kingston.'

The lump in her throat grew bigger. 'I wish I could. But I don't know where he is and I don't know what's going on.' She choked, swallowing back the tears with a huge effort, determined not to break down in front of him. 'But I must get home and find out. You have to let me go!'

'Miss Kingston, we have already established that I'm not letting you go until your brother arrives to take your place.'

Emily stared at him in frustration. 'But if I can't even contact him to tell him that—'

'You're not leaving.' His jaw tightened. 'Doubtless your brother will eventually realize that your plan failed and that you are still in Kazban. Will he have the courage to come here and take your place, I wonder?'

He took a step backwards and her hand fell away from his arm.

'There *was* no plan.' Fighting back tears of frustration, Emily shook her head in disbelief. 'And you are *so* suspicious.'

Did he have no humanity at all?

What did a small sum of money matter when compared to her brother's safety?

What if something had happened to Peter?

'If I am suspicious, then it is with reason.' From behind his back the prince produced the cord that she'd removed from the curtain in her bedroom and she felt her colour rise.

'It was the only way I could find of getting away from the palace,' she mumbled and Zak lifted an eyebrow as he paced towards her.

'You didn't think of using the door?'

She rubbed her toe on the Persian rug. 'You wouldn't have let me leave through a door.'

'I'm not going to let you leave at all.' Zak stared down at her, his wickedly sexy eyes black as pitch. 'There is no possible exit you can take from the palace without being seen. If you escape again I will merely bring you back again, so you might as well accept that fact. You're not leaving here until your brother arrives to take your place. The best thing you can do is pray that your brother realizes the error of his ways and decides to be held accountable for his actions.'

With that he dropped the cord in her lap and walked out of the room, leaving her staring after him feeling utterly helpless.

Emily limped across her enormous bedroom, ignoring the 2800pain in her ankle.

Her guest room was exquisitely decorated and at any other time she would have been open-mouthed with awe at the grandeur of her surroundings but all she could think about was her brother and the fact that Zak al-Farisi obviously wasn't going to let her go.

How *could* he be so unreasonable?

All her instincts told her that Peter wouldn't have taken a holiday at this time and that there was something serious going on. Something that she might be able to help with if she hadn't been stuck in Kazban.

She *had* to do something. But what?

Escaping was proving impossible and the prince obviously didn't have a compassionate bone in his body, so pleading wouldn't work.

And as for that ridiculous conversation about his harem—

Her heart lurched uncomfortably. At the moment she was so desperate that had she thought seduction would work then she'd happily have employed it as a tactic, but she knew absolutely nothing about seduction and she wouldn't have the first clue how to proposition a man even had she wanted to.

She was running through the options in her head when she heard the unmistakable screams of a small child.

Emily winced and glanced at the maid who was preparing her bed for the night. 'Aisha, who is that crying?'

The maid gave a nervous smile. 'It is Jamal, my lady,' she murmured reluctantly. 'The prince's little nephew. He is only five years old and he is very highly strung. Sometimes he has bad dreams—the staff find him difficult.'

Staff?

The screams intensified and Emily felt the tension rise in her. Surely someone was going to stop the child crying? 'So if the staff find him difficult—what about his parents?'

Aisha locked her hands, her features carefully composed. 'His mother is presently abroad, Miss Kingston. She likes to travel.'

'Right.' Emily digested that and told herself firmly that it was absolutely none of her business. She had enough problems in Kazban without encountering any more.

The screams grew more frantic and she clenched her jaw and gave up the fight. She could no more leave a child screaming like that than she could walk naked through the *souk*.

'All right.' She looked at Aisha with exasperation and

limped towards the door. 'So who cuddles him when his mother is away?'

'The young prince has a nanny,' Aisha ventured, frowning slightly as Emily opened the door. 'Miss Kingston, you shouldn't go to him—he's in good hands—'

'Well, it certainly doesn't sound like it,' Emily muttered, 'and if no one else is going to stop that screaming, then I am.'

Without waiting for permission, she walked along the corridor until she located the sound and pushed open the door, her gaze immediately homing in on a little figure in the middle of a huge bed. She looked round the huge room and thought that it was no wonder that the child had nightmares. Cosy it was *not*.

Who on earth had decided that this was a suitable room for a child?

The child sobbed and screamed and a young girl was shouting at him in exasperation, clearly at the end of her tether.

Emily looked at her in disbelief. 'Stop shouting.' She kept her own voice soft so that the tension didn't escalate even further. 'You're making it worse.' Hiding her anger, she gestured for the girl to step backwards. 'You *don't* shout at a child who's upset!'

The girl was breathing heavily, her expression exasperated. 'But he's just so *naughty*—'

Emily raised an eyebrow. 'He's five years old,' she said flatly. 'If he wasn't naughty, I'd be worried.'

The child's screams intensified and he drummed his arms and legs on the bed.

'He's scaring himself. He needs to be cuddled,' Emily said firmly, slipping off her shoes and sliding onto the bed. It was the only way to reach the child. The bed was simply enormous. Having settled herself comfortably, Emily scooped the child onto her lap and cuddled him close, ignoring the flailing arms and the kicking. She hugged him tightly, talked softly to him and finally, just when she was ready to give up and try something else, he gave a sob and flopped against her, exhausted.

Emily let out a breath. 'Gosh, that must have been an awful dream,' she murmured, stroking his hair away from his face with a gentle hand. His face was scarlet and damp from crying and he looked utterly pathetic. 'Do you want to tell me about it?'

'Tigers—' the little boy hiccoughed '—and more tigers.'

Emily frowned and rocked him gently. 'And what were the tigers doing?'

The child gave a jerky breath and snuggled closer. 'Chasing me. They were going to *eat* me. Just like the story.'

Emily felt him shiver and tightened her grip. 'Just like what story?'

'The one that Yasmina read to me.' He looked at the young girl and shrank closer to Emily.

'I see.' Emily glared at the girl, who looked distinctly uncomfortable. Then she glanced around the room. 'Well, there are no tigers here, but it's pretty dark, isn't it? What you need is a light so that there are no dark corners.'

'Mama says that lights are for babies,' he said in a small voice and Emily smiled.

'I like a light on at night. Do I look like a baby to you?'

The little boy stared at her with wide eyes and then shook his head. 'No. You look like a princess.'

'Do you like princesses?'

He nodded and she smiled.

'All right, Jamal, this is what we're going to do. Yasmina here—' she dealt the girl a frosty glance '—is going to organize a light for you and then you and I are going to read a different sort of story. My favourite story.'

He looked at her doubtfully. 'About tigers?'

'Definitely not.' Emily pulled a face to show what she thought of that idea. 'It's about a princess.'

Jamal's face brightened. 'Does she have golden hair like you?'

'Just like me.'

'Is she pretty, like you?'

'Much prettier.'

Jamal looked doubtful. 'All right.' He stuck his thumb in his mouth and looked up at her expectantly.

Yasmina lifted her chin defiantly. 'His Highness does not allow me to leave the child.'

'That's presumably because he's never heard you yelling. You can leave him. I'll take responsibility,' Emily said coldly, her gaze sliding to the little boy on her lap. If the prince thought that she was going to leave the child in the care of a nanny whose idea of a bedtime story scared him witless, then he had another think coming! And if he wanted to throw her in the dungeon for that, then he could feel free. 'If you could fetch me a light and a glass of milk, before you go, that would be great.'

Yasmina backed out of the room and Emily returned her attention to the child.

'OK, Jamal, are you ready for that story?'

CHAPTER FIVE

ZAK stood in the doorway of the room, his eyes on the two figures lying on the bed. They were oblivious to his presence, both totally engrossed in the story. One telling it, one listening.

'And the prince said, "Save me, save me,"' Emily was saying in a soft voice, 'and so the princess climbed up the side of the building and handed him the key that she'd stolen from the guard.'

Jamal's eyes were like saucers. 'Did she kill the guard?'

'Kill?' Emily put a hand to her throat, horrified at the suggestion. 'Goodness, no! The princess was a very kind girl. She used far cleverer ways to get what she wanted.'

Zak gave a cynical smile. Of course she did. Wasn't that what women always did? A sword was much too direct for them. They used other, more devious means of getting their own way.

Like trying to fool the prince with a show of feminine innocence.

'Well, I don't think the prince was very brave. Not like my uncle. He's a proper prince. *Nothing* scares him.'

A small smile touched Zak's mouth at this evidence of uncritical hero-worship.

Emily lifted a hand and stroked the dark head with a gentle hand. 'But I'm sure even your uncle wouldn't use that sword unless he had to.'

Jamal nestled closer to her, clearly enraptured by the story. 'Did the princess in your story have a sword?'

'The princess *hated* violence,' Emily said firmly, her blue eyes twinkling with laughter. 'She used a water pistol.'

A water pistol? Zak struggled not to laugh along with her, his eyes still on the little boy and the woman who was cuddling him.

He'd been intending to sort out the issue of Jamal's nanny earlier in the day but his trip to the *souk* had delayed him, and when he had been informed that the child was screaming he'd prepared himself mentally for a long and difficult evening.

Instead he'd found the child calm and happy and snuggled tightly in the arms of Emily Kingston.

Surprise had rippled through him. That he had *not* expected.

Blissfully unaware of his scrutiny, she was curled up on the bed, happy and relaxed, totally at ease with the child. Against his will, Zak's eyes raked the soft curve of her breast and her rounded hips and he felt an inexplicable surge of lust. Her blonde hair flowed loose over her shoulders and she was still wearing the blue dress, although she'd somehow secured the neckline.

He remembered her comments about his harem and the tension inside him rose to almost intolerable levels. If he *had* a harem then she would now be lying flat on a bed awaiting his pleasure and he would be preparing himself for a long and *extremely* satisfying night.

Jamal gave a yawn. 'I like that story, but I still think that the prince is supposed to do the rescuing. My uncle would *never* need anyone to rescue him,' he said in a sleepy voice and Zak's eyes narrowed as he watched Emily smile.

'No?' she murmured. 'Well, princes don't always behave the way you think they should. Sometimes they can surprise you.'

'I think the princess was very clever,' Jamal murmured, his eyes drifting shut, and Emily shifted slightly so that she could pull a blanket over him.

She lay next to him, stroking his hair until she was sure that he was asleep.

Zak frowned slightly as he observed her patience and gentleness with the child. Aware that most people struggled to handle Jamal, he was surprised by how easily she'd calmed him and built a relationship within a ridiculously short space of time.

But then he already knew that she was clever. Look how hard she was working to convince him of her innocence.

Satisfied that the child was asleep, the girl wriggled gently away from him and slid off the bed.

Zak noticed that this time she was barefoot, the bandage the only evidence of her earlier brush with danger in the *souk*. He moved, treading silently as he strolled across the rug towards her. 'A *water* pistol?'

She gasped in fright and covered her mouth with her hand. 'Oh, you made me jump!' She cast an anxious look at the child. '*Don't* wake him up! It's taken me ages to settle him.'

'I'm aware of that,' Zak said dryly, noticing that without her ridiculous heels she barely reached his shoulder. She also looked very, very young. Gritting his teeth, he reminded himself just what she was. *A woman who sanctioned theft on a grand scale.* A woman who was hotly sexual and not afraid to display such passions. Young, she might be, but innocent she was not. 'I understand he had a bad dream again?'

'Again?' She frowned up at him. 'It's happened before?'

Zak stared down at his little nephew. 'It happens all the time.'

'Well, you should start by firing that nanny! She's awful!'

'The nanny has already given her notice.'

'You should be grateful for that! She read him a story about tigers eating little boys!' She glared at him as though he'd been personally responsible for the misjudgment. 'I mean, how ridiculous can you get? And when he was crying she was shouting at him. It's no wonder the child is scared of the dark—the woman is freaky. How long has she been his nanny?'

Zak tensed. 'Less than a month.'

'A *month*?' She looked startled. 'And the one before that? How long did she last?'

'Two weeks.' Zak gritted his teeth as he read the amusement in her eyes. 'It is *not* funny.'

She clamped her lips together but he saw the tiny dimple appear by the side of her mouth. 'I disagree. When a five year old runs the household, it's funny.'

'He is a difficult child.'

'Of course he is,' she muttered, her eyes sliding to the child who still slept. 'If I had a different carer every few weeks, I'd make sure I was difficult too.'

Zak's eyes narrowed. 'What are you saying?'

'Children need consistency. And Jamal doesn't have any. He's horrifically insecure and it's no wonder he has bad dreams.'

'And you worked all that out in one short evening?' Unaccustomed to being in a position where he felt forced to defend himself, Zak felt a surge of irritation. 'Jamal does have consistency,' he growled. 'The palace is teeming with his family. And the place is crawling with guards. He can hardly feel threatened.'

The implied slur on his family touched his pride and he folded his arms across his chest and stared at her, subjecting her to the full force of his gaze.

She stared right back. 'Children need a special person to bond with. And it is his imagination that threatens him,' she said quietly, 'not the reality. And, yes, I've worked it out in one short evening. I'm used to children of Jamal's age. It's my job and I'm well qualified, which I suspect is more than can be said for that girl who was terrifying the life out of him.'

Adjusting rapidly to the realization that there might actually be more to Emily Kingston than met the eye, Zak caught the accusation in her gaze and tensed. 'His mother selects his nannies—'

'This is the same mother who leaves him alone?' She

blurted the words out and then had the grace to blush. 'I—I'm sorry. It's none of my business.'

Zak was silent for a long moment and then decided that he could not defend the indefensible. 'No. You're right.' His voice was tight. 'My sister-in-law has never taken her responsibilities seriously enough. And I have not interfered as much as I should have done.'

And there were good reasons for that.

Wondering what was driving him to reveal intimate family matters to a total stranger, Zak rubbed a hand over the back of his neck to relieve some of the tension, aware that she was looking at him with a puzzled expression on her lovely face.

'But why should you interfere? You're not the child's father. Surely that's your brother's responsibility.'

'My brother is dead, Miss Kingston.'

He saw the shock in her eyes and he withdrew, carefully masking his expression. This conversation had most *definitely* gone far enough.

'I'm sorry.' Her voice was quiet. 'That's terrible. Poor Jamal. And poor you. You lost your brother.'

Poor you?

Since his brother's untimely death not one single other person had dared utter words of such a personal nature and Zak tensed as emotions that he'd resolutely refused to acknowledge surged through his powerful frame.

She knew nothing of the circumstances of Raschid's death and he had no intention of sharing the information with her.

'It is not something that is discussed.' His tone was forbidding but she just looked at him with that clear blue gaze that he found so disconcerting.

Others bowed or averted their eyes in his presence. The fact that Emily Kingston forgot or refused to do either was at the same time irritating and refreshing.

'I know how hard it can be to lose someone you love,' she said softly and he sucked in a breath in a hiss.

'Before you shed tears over that which you know nothing, I should inform you that my brother died when Jamal was still so little, he has no real sense of loss.'

'I was talking about *your* loss.'

The tension in his shoulders reflected his supreme discomfort. 'I do not need, or wish for, your sympathy.'

She nodded. 'Of course you don't. Men are always hopeless at showing their emotions.'

He gritted his teeth. 'Self-discipline is a quality to be valued highly and this is not a conversation that I wish to pursue.' Swiftly he steered the subject into safer waters. 'So if you're such an expert on children, tell me what to do about the nightmares.'

In truth he felt responsible for his little nephew, knowing that his sister-in law was a frivolous, hard-hearted woman with no thought for anyone but herself. And he was truly disturbed to think that the child was having bad dreams. Making up his mind that the nanny would be dealt with severely, he looked at her expectantly.

'Well, the first thing I'd do is move him. This room is totally unsuitable for a child who has bad dreams. It's hardly surprising that this room scares him. It's—*huge*.' She waved a hand around her to illustrate her point. 'It has lots of scary corners that create shadows. He ought to be in a bright, cheerful bedroom with painted animals on the walls and a good nightlight that shows everything for what it is.'

Zak glanced around the room, trying for the first time ever to look at it through a child's eyes. 'It was chosen by his mother.'

'Does the size of the room reflect the status of the person in Kazban?'

She was unusually observant, Zak reflected.

His sister-in-law had indeed chosen the room for its size rather than its appeal to a child. But then everything Danielle did was measured in terms of status. A child's comfort would have meant nothing to her when making her choice of rooms.

He made an instant decision. 'First thing tomorrow we will move Jamal. You will choose the room.'

She gaped at him. 'Me?'

'Why not?' He gave an indolent shrug. 'You have professed yourself an expert on these matters and Jamal clearly likes you.'

'Well—' her eyes slid to Jamal, who was still sleeping soundly on the bed '—all right. And while you're at it, you need to employ a decent nanny. Someone who isn't going to leave or read him stories that give him nightmares.'

Zak looked at her thoughtfully, an idea forming in his mind. 'Since you're so sure what the child needs, you can also fulfil that role for the time being,' he said smoothly, seeing an instant solution to a problem that had been nagging him for some time. Her morals might be extremely questionable but there was no denying that she'd taken good care of Jamal that evening.

'Me?' She was looking at him with an appalled expression on her face. 'I can't do it! As soon as Peter comes, I'm going home.'

'But I think we've both established that he isn't coming, is he, Miss Kingston?' Zak smiled. He had to give her full marks for perseverance. 'Or perhaps you are worried that caring for Jamal will interfere with your next escape plan. What will it be tomorrow, I wonder?' he drawled softly, stepping closer and watching the way her lips parted and her breathing quickened. 'Will you be using water pistols at dawn?'

She glared at him, but he saw the betraying colour in her cheeks and the way her eyes drifted to his mouth.

She was remembering the kiss. And so was he.

White-hot lust thudded through his body and he was about to drag her into his arms and give way to temptation when he remembered Jamal.

He gritted his teeth in frustration.

Was he fated to *always* be in public with this woman?

Seriously tempted to resurrect the institution of the harem just so that he could place her in it and pay regular visits, Zak let his eyes drift over her smooth cheeks and rest on her soft mouth. It still infuriated him that, even though his brain knew she was duplicitous and had no morals, his body was more than happy to seek the most intimate acquaintance possible.

But perhaps that just proved that, in spite of everything that had happened, he was still capable of feeling some emotion, albeit only on a physical level.

He was a healthy adult male with strong sexual appetites. Despite all her claims to innocence, she made no secret of the fact that she wanted him. It was written in her every glance. And presumably that was her intention. He watched as she dragged her eyes away from his mouth, her cheeks slightly flushed. How did she do that? he wondered. Contrive to appear so innocent?

'I-I'm really sorry that I can't stay to sort out your nanny crisis,' she stammered, backing away from him slightly, 'but I really have to get home to my own brother.'

'But your brother isn't *at* home, is he?' Zak pointed out silkily. 'So until you've identified his current whereabouts, there is little point in even thinking of leaving Kazban.'

Her eyes flickered hesitantly to his again and their eyes locked. Heat and awareness flared between them and Zak felt raw desire rip through his body.

Assuring himself that his nephew was in a deep and peaceful sleep, he hauled her against him and brought his mouth down on hers with crushing force. Her soft lips instantly parted and she leaned into him, sliding her arms around his neck to bring herself closer.

He tasted the sweetness of her mouth, felt the curve of her hip pressing against him, and suddenly his whole body was on fire.

He felt her teeth on his bottom lip and then the gentle touch of her tongue, soothing and seducing. Driven by the almost unbearable ache in his groin, he captured her face with his hands and held her firm so that he could explore her mouth in minute detail.

Her body was shivering against his and he felt the warmth of her skin through the fabric of her dress. She was all feminine temptation and torment and heat licked through his veins, driving him wild.

A sound from the bed brought him back to the present and he lifted his head, once again appalled by his need to have this woman no matter what the consequences.

Her eyes were glazed, unfocused, and she swayed forward again, her gaze fixed longingly on his mouth.

With a huge effort of will, he forced himself to release her, backing away from her as if she were a poisonous snake.

Wrestling with emotions that he hadn't experienced since he was a hormonal teenager, Zak strode out of the room without a backward glance, cursing the fact that Peter Kingston had ever decided to do business with the state of Kazban.

Emily replaced the receiver with a shaking hand.

Still there was no answer from Peter's home and no clue at all as to why he would have taken off without telling anyone where he was going. It was so unlike him and suddenly she wondered just how well she knew her own brother.

Soaked with anxiety, she stared mindlessly out of the window and then gave a frown as she suddenly became aware of the commotion in the courtyard below.

The prince's black stallion was rampaging round the yard, scattering servants in his wake. Thoroughly overexcited and extremely bad tempered, his teeth were bared and he kicked out at anyone who came close to him.

Emily watched, transfixed, and then suddenly her attention was caught by a tiny figure in the corner of the yard, walking forwards, hand outstretched to the enormous horse.

Jamal!

'Oh, no—' Filled with foreboding, Emily turned to the young girl who'd been sent to her with a selection of clothes. 'Which way?' she demanded urgently. 'How do I get to that courtyard?'

She needed to get down there before the child was killed!

The girl glanced at her nervously and then hurried to the door and pointed to a set of stairs.

'At the bottom is a door that opens directly onto the courtyard,' she said and Emily flew past her without further delay, driven by anxiety for the child.

It was obvious to her that the servants had no intention of going near the horse, which meant that no one was going to stop Jamal from putting himself in the path of the stallion.

Sahara was up to his tricks again.

Dark eyes veiled by thick lashes, Zak watched from his office in exasperated amusement as his favourite stallion defeated all attempts to capture him, his nostrils flaring and his eyes wild as he reared up in the yard, scattering the stable staff.

Someone obviously hadn't locked the stable door properly, Zak thought wearily, reflecting that if his staff were as clever as his horse then they might do a lot better.

But whatever the reason, the horse was now loose in the yard and no one had the nerve to get too close.

Deciding that the time had come to return the animal to the stud farm where he could gallop to his heart's content, Zak realized that he'd better get down to the yard before the horse hurt someone.

Abandoning the paperwork that had accumulated in his absence, he rose to his feet in a fluid movement and then stopped, paralyzed by the sight of his little nephew walking towards the horse.

Frozen to the spot, Zak waited for one of the servants to extract the child from danger, but they were chattering nervously among themselves, each too concerned about his own safety to worry about the child.

Fear, like a lead weight, settled in Zak's insides.

The gravity of the situation was immediately obvious and he prepared himself to witness a hideous accident because he knew that, no matter how quickly he moved, there was no way he would be able to reach the child in time.

And then he saw another figure crossing the courtyard, long blonde hair tumbling down her back as she moved swiftly towards the child. Without hesitation, she reached out in a decisive movement and scooped Jamal out of harm's way, thrusting him bodily into the arms of one of the servants who was hovering at a safe distance.

Zak hadn't even been aware that he was holding his breath until he found himself releasing it slowly. The immediate danger averted, gradually his heart rate returned to normal and he waited to see the woman retreat to the safety of the palace. Instead she turned her head and spoke to the servant who held Jamal, waiting while he took the little boy to safety. Then she turned back to the horse, her intentions clear.

Zak cursed softly under his breath. Far from being resolved, the situation had returned to critical because by now Sahara had become bored and impatient and was baring his teeth, his expression dangerous.

And this time the victim would be the girl.

He sucked in a breath, the tension spreading through his powerful shoulders as he watched her approach the horse. *Didn't she know the risk?*

No one had ever been able to handle Sahara except him.

This time Zak moved, making it down to the courtyard in

record time, but not quickly enough to prevent Emily Kingston from walking towards his stallion.

He gritted his teeth, afraid to call out in case he startled the horse.

A chill ran through him as he contemplated just how much damage an enraged Arabian stallion could cause to one slender female.

He might not *like* the woman but he most certainly didn't want her death on his conscience.

With a muttered oath he relieved the nearest guard of his gun, feeling a sickness deep in his stomach. He prayed that he wouldn't have to shoot the horse that he'd bred himself and nurtured from a colt. But if he had to, then—

Ignoring the excitement and panic of the stable staff, the girl strolled forward slowly, talking to the horse as if he were a friend and they were having a conversation.

Zak saw the horse tense suspiciously. Realizing that she was now so close to the animal that any movement on his part could put her in danger, Zak held himself still, watching through narrowed eyes as she spoke quietly to the horse.

'You're a great big bully,' she said in a conversational tone, 'frightening everyone like that. You've got to learn to play nicely if you're going to have any friends.'

Zak's fingers tightened on the gun and he braced himself, waiting for Sahara to display his natural instincts to kill everyone who approached him. Instead the horse gave a disgusted snort and butted the girl with his nose.

She smiled and let him smell her. 'You don't deserve anything to eat because you've been naughty,' she told him firmly, lifting a hand and rubbing the side of Sahara's neck gently. 'But when you learn some manners, I'll give you something nice to eat.'

Sahara gave another snort and Zak let out a breath, staggered that she was still alive. He watched in stunned amazement as she slid her hand over the horse, her touch almost sensual as she smoothed Sahara's strong neck.

The horse turned his head and blew gently on her hand and Zak shook his head in incredulous disbelief.

Was she some sort of sorceress?

No one was able to get that close to Sahara, except him.

And here she was rubbing the animal's nose and telling him off as if he were a tame donkey.

It seemed that even Sahara was susceptible to her feminine charms.

Zak gave a cynical laugh. Not satisfied with seducing *him*, the woman was now trying to seduce his horse.

And it seemed to be working.

The tension had left the horse and he stood, docile and contented, allowing himself to be petted.

'You're so handsome,' she crooned softly, stepping closer still and rubbing the horse's neck until the animal gave a whicker and nudged her pockets hopefully.

'Oh, go on, then,' she said indulgently. 'Just a few mints.'

She reached into her pocket and pulled something out, feeding it to the horse, who munched happily, butting her with his nose in gratitude.

'One day I'm going to ride you,' she murmured and Zak felt anger surge through him, fuelled by the relief that no one had been hurt.

'Don't even think about it,' he said coldly, thrusting the gun back into the hands of the nearest guard and walking towards them. He shook his head in exasperation. 'Are you now trying to escape my palace in an ambulance? Or was that heroic performance another elaborate trick on your part to persuade me to release you?'

'Trick?' For a moment she looked puzzled and then understanding dawned and her blue eyes shone with incredulity. 'You think I *pushed* Jamal in front of that horse especially so that I could then rescue him? Are you sick?'

'What I think, Miss Kingston,' he said icily, 'is that you would do whatever it takes to secure your release. And it seems to me that putting me in your debt would appear to be a possible way of achieving that objective.'

'Stop talking like a businessman and start thinking like a human,' she suggested, her tone equally cold. 'I would *never* put a child in danger and the fact that you even *think* that I might shows me that you know nothing whatsoever about me.'

'Why else would you risk your life for a child with whom you have no blood tie, if not for personal gain?'

She gaped at him and appeared temporarily speechless. When she finally found her voice it was croaky. 'Because I would never let anything happen to another person if I was able to prevent it.'

'So the fact that I am now in your debt is of no relevance to you.'

'You're not in my debt.' She looked him straight in the eye. 'I didn't do what I did for you. In fact it might surprise you to know that I wasn't even thinking about you at the time.'

She was so outraged by the suggestion that for the first time in years Zak felt a flicker of uncertainty.

But to have believed her would have meant believing that she'd committed an act of total selflessness and he knew that few, if any, women were capable of such goodness. Certainly not a woman like Emily Kingston, who dismissed the loss of people's savings with such casual ease.

'You and your brother are little more than thieves,' he drawled softly, 'so you must forgive me if I take a little convincing regarding your motives for that seemingly heroic rescue.'

He was prepared to believe that she might not have actually engineered the incident, but that didn't change the fact that she'd taken full advantage of the situation that had presented itself.

'Let's get one thing straight, shall we?' She put her hands on her hips and Sahara threw up his head in alarm. 'Sooner or later Peter is going to repay the money he owes you and then you are going to have to admit that you were wrong. Frankly, I can't wait for the apology.'

Unaccustomed to being challenged on any point, least of all one that was supported by a substantial body of evidence, Zak sucked in a breath, anger rising in him like lava in a volcano.

With an imperious flick of one bronzed hand he dismissed the servants, resolving to deal with their cowardice in not helping Jamal at some later date.

At the moment his attention was focused on Emily Kingston, and as he boxed the stallion and secured the bolt Zak gritted his teeth and decided that he'd had enough of her games.

His fingers closed around her slim wrist and he held her in an iron grasp. 'Come with me. We end this. Now.'

CHAPTER SIX

END what?

What was Zak talking about?

Wincing slightly as his fingers bit into her wrist, Emily virtually had to run to keep up with him as he strode purposefully along the marbled corridors of the palace, scattering servants and guards in his wake.

Finally they reached his office and he flung open the door and dragged her inside.

Totally stunned by his behaviour, she stared at him in amazement and no small degree of trepidation. 'What is this all about?' She jumped slightly as the door slammed shut.

'I think we should both stop playing games, Miss Kingston. Your continued denial that there is anything wrong offends me deeply.' He reached for a pile of papers and handed them to her. 'Read! Perhaps then we can drop this pretence that you are innocent and that everyone is going to live happily ever after. Let us both finally agree that your life is no fairy tale.'

Looking at the grim set of his mouth, something shifted inside her. *What exactly was he talking about?* With a sense of foreboding Emily stared at the papers in her hand, wondering what they contained. With a final glance at Zak, she bent her head and leafed through the papers slowly, a feeling of dread spreading through her body.

What did it all mean?

Pages and pages of figures swam in front of her eyes, together with incomprehensible legal jargon that made no sense at all.

Emily went back to the beginning and started again, this time concentrating hard on what she was reading, looking for the important bits. She found a summary and read that, and as she reached the end the papers slipped from her fingers and floated onto the floor.

No—

'These papers say that my brother embezzled the money,' she whispered, her whole body suddenly frozen with shock. 'They say that he never invested a penny.'

'That's correct.' Zak watched her through narrowed eyes and then stooped in a lithe movement and retrieved the papers. 'And now that you are finally aware that I know the truth, I think your best course of action would be to drop the show of innocence. I have a great appreciation for honesty and so far you have displayed none whatsoever.'

Emily ignored him, too shattered by the enormity of what she'd just discovered to even attempt a response. She wasn't listening to him.

Peter had *taken* the money?

'Eight million pounds,' she whispered to herself. 'He took eight *million* pounds.' Her legs were shaking so badly that she leaned against the desk, needing physical support. As if in a dream, she ran through what she'd just read and tried to match it with what she already knew about her brother.

'I need more time, Em—'

'If I go, Em, I'll be thrown into jail—'

'Oh, my God.' Emily covered her mouth with a shaking hand, feeling as though someone had injected icy water into her veins. No wonder Peter had been worried about being imprisoned. 'He took the money and he lost it.'

And with that realization, Emily did something she'd never done before.

She fainted.

How was it that women always managed to faint when things became difficult?

Was it a skill that they taught in school?

With a sigh of impatience, Zak stooped and lifted her,

rying not to notice the soft curves of her body as he carried
her to the couch. This time she was limp in his arms, her
blonde hair trailing over his arm like a waterfall. All traces
of colour had drained from her cheeks and he felt a mo-
mentary flash of concern.

Then he remembered his sister-in law's ability to faint at
will, a skill that had always stood her in good stead.

Emily Kingston had obviously perfected the same art, he
thought grimly. Finding it impossible to continue to claim
ignorance of her brother's misdeeds, she was forced to find
another means to escape responsibility.

Her eyes flickered open and he stared into deep pools of
blue, clouded with confusion and anxiety.

She looked tiny and delicate lying on his sofa and once
again Zak found himself fighting the temptation to take her
in his arms and offer protection, but fortunately the scars of
his past throbbed warningly and he took a step backwards.

He was *not* so much of a fool as to allow himself to be
manipulated by the amazing acting skills of one extremely
guilty woman.

Ruthlessly determined to squash her feminine games, he
summoned the servants and ordered that a doctor be called
immediately to his office, entirely convinced that a medical
examination would confirm his belief that she was faking.

The room filled with people and the doctor returned, bowing and scraping as Zak paced the room impatiently, waiting
to be told that Emily Kingston was, in fact, in excellent
health.

As the minutes ticked by and the doctor continued what
seemed like a ridiculously lengthy examination he became
more and more exasperated.

Exactly how long did it take to spot a fraud?

Finally the doctor rose to his feet, his expression per-
turbed. 'She has evidently received an unpleasant shock.'
The doctor ran through the various findings of his examination and Zak ground his teeth with irritation. An irritation

that increased radically when the doctor suggested that she remain on his sofa for the next few hours and not be moved under any circumstances.

Zak glared at the man with naked incredulity, attempting to recall the qualifications that had persuaded him to appoint him as one of the team of doctors who were permanently available for the use of his family and the palace staff.

Was the man really suggesting that the faint was genuine?

Before he could speak, Emily Kingston struggled into a sitting position, her blue eyes huge in her white face.

'I'm all right—really. I'm sorry to be such a bother.'

The doctor gave her a fatherly smile and patted her arm in a reassuring way, a gesture that irritated Zak still further

Was he the only one who saw through her?

Of course she'd received a shock.

The shock of knowing that he had evidence against her brother.

The shock of knowing that her pretence of innocence was no longer going to work.

One of the servants placed a tray next to her, loaded with water, strong coffee and dates, but she just looked at it blankly and then lifted her eyes to Zak.

'I—I need to talk to you.'

Zak gave a cynical smile. Of course she needed to talk to him. The innocent act was no longer viable so now she would have to find a different way to manipulate him. Doubtless her fainting act had bought her some time and she was now prepared to embark on a new course of persuasion

Given the kisses they'd exchanged and the longing looks she'd been casting in his direction, he prepared himself for an *extremely* improper suggestion.

Suddenly his body throbbed with expectation.

Deciding that their next conversation would be best conducted in private, Zak dismissed the servants and the doctor with one snap of his fingers and waited for the door to close behind them. 'Perhaps you should take some refreshment. You look a little pale.'

His sarcastic tone seemed lost on her.

'I couldn't possibly eat a thing,' she mumbled, raking her blonde hair away from her face with a shaky hand. She frowned, as if she were trying to work something out. 'I've never fainted before in my life. I can't think what happened.'

'You were in a tricky situation,' Zak observed helpfully, 'and such a skill always provides a useful escape route.'

Her mouth opened and closed and she looked at him with a lack of comprehension. 'You're suggesting that I did it on *purpose*?'

'You were healthy enough to throw yourself in front of my stallion less than half an hour ago,' Zak pointed out brutally, observing the continuing drain of colour from her cheeks with no small degree of fascination, 'which precludes any serious physical cause for your sudden desire to fall at my feet. I really ought to try it myself. You wouldn't believe the tedium of some of the official functions I attend.'

There was a long silence as she looked at him in puzzled disbelief. 'Who was she?'

Totally thrown by her unexpected response, Zak's eyes suddenly narrowed warily. 'Who was who?'

'The woman who made you so cynical.' Ignoring the doctor's instructions, she struggled to her feet, swayed slightly and then lifted a hand to ward him off as he took an automatic step forward. 'You believe that everyone is playing some sort of elaborate—g-game, designed to deceive you. Well, I don't play games, Your Highness. Stay away from me. You may be a prince, but you don't have an ounce of human kindness in you. I don't want you to touch me.'

Retaining an uncomfortably vivid recollection of her passionate response to the last time he'd touched her, Zak lifted an eyebrow, his gaze faintly mocking. 'No?'

She turned away from him, holding onto the arm of the sofa for support. 'No! And if you're thinking about that kiss, well, let's just say that you caught me at a weak moment and you're a good kisser. I dare say you've had plenty of practice,' she muttered and Zak gritted his teeth, exasperated by the fact that she was actually managing to make *him* feel guilty.

'There was more than one kiss—'

'Let's get back to Peter.' She stared at him, the accusation in her eyes keeping him at arm's length. 'You knew, didn' you? You knew that Peter had embezzled the money. That's what this is all about.'

'Of course I knew.' Zak looked at her impatiently. 'That is why I ordered him to attend the meeting. And that is why he sent you in his place. You knew, too—'

'No!' Her sharp denial made him tense with shock.

No one ever spoke to him in that tone. He was used to people who fawned and anticipated his every whim. Especially women. And here she was, arguing and challenging him in a way that was totally without precedent.

'I *didn't* know.' She barely reached his shoulder and yet the flash of her eyes and the lift of her chin gave her sudden stature. 'I thought that my brother had made some investments which had failed to produce the expected return. I thought he would pay them back soon. I *told* you that.'

But he hadn't believed her.

And he didn't believe her now.

Zak was silent for a moment. 'Your brother spent some time working for a bank in Kazban. During that time he persuaded honest citizens to part with their savings and trust him to invest in various stock options. He was supposed to make the investments on their behalf,' he said finally, wondering why he was spelling out what she knew already, 'but instead he took the money for himself.'

She stared at him with growing horror. 'And that's what you meant.' She shook her head slowly. 'That first day when you said that a family could starve, that was what you meant.'

Zak ground his teeth, wishing she would just confess that she'd known about the enormity of the debt all along so that they could end this charade. 'You knew that he had taken savings from the people of Kazban—'

She sank back down on the couch, her hands clenched into fists. 'He told me it was *you*.' Her voice was barely a whisper. 'He told me that he'd made some investments for *you*.'

Zak frowned. 'In the event that is what has happened,' he said curtly. 'Those people would have suffered significant hardship had I not intervened. I have chosen to repay his debt.'

She lifted her gaze to his and her eyes were dull. 'I'm sure you're just a saint.'

Unaccustomed to being on the receiving end of sarcasm, Zak struggled for a suitable response. 'I have acted with honour.'

'Honour?' She gave an incredulous laugh. 'You have accused me of something of which I am totally innocent. You thought I knew all about the debt. You thought I was part of a big cover up. A plan to escape responsibility.'

Zak breathed in deeply, shards of colour touching his hard cheekbones as he inclined his head. That was exactly what he'd thought and it was nothing less than the truth, so why would he not admit it? And why were her eyes loaded with accusation?

Her eyes closed. Long, thick lashes brushed her pale cheeks and for a brief moment he thought he saw something glisten on those lashes. But then she opened her eyes and looked straight at him.

'I don't know where Peter is, but I do know that there must be a good reason for all this. Peter is good and kind and he never stole anything from anybody in his life.'

Zak stared at her. The evidence was laid before her and yet she *still* defended her brother. For a brief moment he felt a flicker of admiration. Whatever her sins, at the very least you had to credit the woman with loyalty.

Something that had been sadly lacking in his *own* brother.

'I see now why you wouldn't let me go. It's an enormous sum of money,' she whispered, staring down at the papers still scattered on the floor. 'It just never occurred to me—' She lifted her head and looked at him, her face ashen. 'Why? Why would he need that much money? What's he done with it? Do you know?'

Zak contemplated her thoughtfully. 'Not yet.'

She gave a humourless laugh. 'But you will. You're looking for him, aren't you?' She wrapped her arms around her slim body and he noticed that, despite the heat, she was shivering.

'Eight million pounds is a considerable sum of money, Miss Kingston,' he said smoothly. 'I have had people looking for him since the day you stepped off the plane at Kazban in your brother's place.'

She gave a painful smile. 'And I can hardly blame you for that. He owes you a fortune.' She was silent for a minute and then she lifted her chin, meeting his gaze bravely. 'Peter took the money and was afraid to face you for whatever reason, so he sent me instead. That was wrong of him. And I can see why you would have believed that I was part of it.'

'And you're saying that you weren't?' His unshakeable belief that she was as guilty as sin wavered in the face of her obvious distress and he had to remind himself that women always used emotion when they were in a tight spot.

'What was Peter thinking of?' She seemed to be talking to herself rather than him. 'He just told me that the investments hadn't gone well—'

'He never made the investments.'

She winced and her face lost the last of its colour. 'I understand that now.' There was a long silence and then she opened her eyes and looked at him. 'And I understand why

ou wouldn't let me leave. We owe you an enormous sum
f money. And there's no way we can even begin to repay
.'

We?

Finally she was taking responsibility for her brother's
ebt?

She looked immensely vulnerable and Zak's mouth tight-
ned. Whether she'd known about her brother's misdeeds,
r not, was irrelevant. What mattered now was the future.

Looking at those amazing blue eyes, the soft mouth and
he swell of her breasts against her shirt, Zak suddenly found
imself reaching a decision about her future with supersonic
peed.

'I know exactly how you can repay it.' He delivered the
vords with the arrogant assurance of someone offering the
ltimate prize. 'You will marry me.'

imily sat on the sofa in a state of shock.

There was an extended silence while she tried several dif-
erent ways to interpret his words. 'Sorry?'

Zak frowned impatiently, clearly unaccustomed to repeat-
ng himself. 'You will marry me,' he said emphatically, his
lark eyes gleaming with a satisfaction that she found im-
ossible to comprehend. 'It is the perfect solution for every-
ne.'

Emily stared, her heart thumping steadily. 'Why would
ou possibly want to marry me?'

'I need a wife,' he said calmly, delivering that statement
n a tone more suited to announcing changes in the stock
narket. 'It is time. It would be a business arrangement, nat-
rally.'

Naturally.

The dreams melted away and Emily scolded herself for
ven expecting to hear anything different.

She was letting a few hot kisses fuel her imagination.

'Right.' She gave a wan smile. 'Well, that's romantic.'

He frowned sharply. 'We are not talking about romance.'

'Obviously not.'

'Remember your fairy tales,' he urged silkily, gripping the tops of her arms with both hands and giving her a little shake. 'You get to marry the prince. What more could you want?'

Love?

'We've been reading different fairy tales,' she said flatly, and he gave an all-male shrug that clearly dismissed the detail.

'This is a modern version.'

'Maybe I have a defective memory,' she muttered, 'but I don't remember a single fairy tale where the prince marries the girl because the clock is ticking. That's a new one.'

'There will be enormous benefits for you,' he volunteered generously, and she looked at him, wondering how there could possibly be a benefit to marrying a man who didn't love her.

'Offhand, I can't think of any.'

'You will have access to enormous wealth.'

'I don't care about money. Money just causes problems.'

Surprise flickered in those dark eyes but, with the ease of a skilled negotiator, he swiftly changed tack. 'My father will give you the title of princess. From the day of our marriage you will be permitted to walk by my side.'

Emily glanced down at his long, powerful legs. 'Generally I can't keep up with you—you walk too fast.'

He gritted his teeth. '*Why* are you joking about this?'

'Because you can't possibly be serious.'

'I am deadly serious and you should know that I have *never* offered marriage to a woman before.'

Realizing that she was supposed to feel honoured by that announcement, Emily frowned. 'Well, you didn't exactly offer it to me,' she pointed out. 'You sort of ordered me to marry you. ''You will marry me,'' were your exact words.'

I suppose you think that you're such a catch that nothing would induce a girl to refuse.'

'I will cancel your brother's debt,' he replied immediately, displaying all the cool purpose of a man intent on bringing a difficult business negotiation to a speedy and satisfactory conclusion.

His words silenced her more effectively than a gag. She opened her mouth and closed it again.

'You would *cancel* the debt?'

'Yes.'

'But he owes you eight million pounds.'

'On the day of our marriage that debt would be erased.'

Eight million pounds. *Eight million pounds.* She stared at him, mute. 'You'd pay that much money to marry me?'

'I need a wife.'

She bit her lip, watching reality involved in a head on collision with her dreams. All her life she'd treasured a vision of a future where she found a man she loved and married him. Never had she thought she'd marry for any other reason than love.

But that was before she'd discovered that her brother was in debt to the tune of eight million pounds. *And before she'd exchanged hot kisses with Zak al-Farisi.*

She swallowed hard, trying to hang onto her principles. 'I need to think about it.'

'That is not possible.' He was arrogantly sure of himself. 'This is a one-time offer. I need to speak to my father today.'

'Are you always this ruthless when it comes to getting what you want?'

He frowned slightly. 'You are, in effect, getting eight million pounds and a lifestyle beyond your wildest dreams. I do not exactly see you suffering from the deal.'

'That's because you don't know anything about my wildest dreams,' she mumbled, realizing just how cynical he was about relationships. He obviously never expected to fall in love, therefore a marriage that was nothing more than a business deal was perfectly acceptable to him.

Whereas she—

Emily swallowed hard. Her wildest dreams had included a cosy home, a gorgeous man and at least five little replicas of that gorgeous man running round their pretty orchard. Never in those dreams had she seen piles of money or gilded palaces.

But neither had she dreamed about the wild passion she'd experienced the night before. It was as if he'd uncovered a part of her that she hadn't known existed.

She looked into Zak's handsome face, looking for the slightest trace of gentleness, but his eyes glittered hard and his mouth was set in a grim line.

'You don't even like me,' she whispered, but even as she said the words their eyes locked together and the burning in her body intensified to almost unbearable proportions, fuelled by the powerful connection between them.

'I don't like your lack of morals, but fortunately for what I have in mind a lack of morals is a distinct advantage.' A flicker of a smile touched that firm mouth. 'You are a stunningly beautiful woman. And I will certainly *like* you when you're lying naked in my bed.'

Emily felt her limbs tremble as his eyes slid over her in blatant masculine appreciation. Heat flared in her pelvis, her whole body reacting as though he'd already touched her.

She shouldn't be feeling like this.

She should leave.

But how could she leave when Peter owed this man a shockingly large sum of money that would surely never be paid back?

Once Crown Prince Zakour al-Farisi tracked him down, he would be thrown into jail.

'I can't believe you'd really want me to—I mean…' She stumbled over the words, painfully embarrassed. She'd never had this sort of conversation with anyone before. 'You say this would be a business arrangement—not a real marriage.'

'What is a real marriage? Among my people, such deals are commonplace.' He gave a dismissive shrug. 'But, in every sense that matters, the marriage would be real.'

Her cheeks flamed. 'I don't understand—'

One dark eyebrow swooped upwards. 'You are incredibly beautiful and I have a high sex drive,' he drawled. 'What's not to understand?'

A high sex drive—

Suddenly her limbs felt weak and she was glad that she was already sitting down.

She just couldn't believe that they were having this conversation.

'All this outraged feminine modesty is totally unnecessary,' he said smoothly. 'I like the fact that you're a passionate woman. And I like the fact that you can't hide the fact that you want me.'

Emily blushed scarlet, just *mortified* that she'd been so obvious.

'You're very good-looking,' she mumbled finally, keeping her gaze fixed firmly on the rug under her feet. 'You must be used to women staring at you.'

'I wasn't complaining.' He sounded amused. 'Merely pointing out that you want me as much as I want you, and I'm perfectly all right with that. I can be very modern in my approach to sex. I don't expect or want a virgin in my bed so you can drop the show of outraged innocence.'

This time she did look at him, her eyes wide with alarm and consternation. 'But—you're saying that if I—if we—' her voice cracked and she closed her eyes briefly, wondering how she was ever going to perform in his bed if she couldn't even manage to talk about the idea without blushing '—if we—do it—then—'

'*Do it?*' His dark eyes glittered as he surveyed her with amusement. '*Do it?* You sound like a schoolgirl.'

She *felt* like a schoolgirl. It obviously hadn't occurred to him that she might be a virgin and she was certainly not going to tell him. She couldn't even *begin* to have such a personal conversation.

'So you're saying that if we—marry—' she licked dry lips '—you'll drop the criminal charges against Peter and cancel the debt?'

'Why not?' He leaned against his desk, arrogantly confident and in control, surveying her through lowered lids. 'It seems a perfectly satisfactory solution all round.'

'You're throwing away a fortune.'

He gave a slow smile that set her nerve endings on fire. 'But I will be gaining a wife and I will be gaining you in my bed,' he said softly, thick dark lashes shielding his expression. 'And at the moment I'm prepared to pay almost any price for that pleasure.'

Her heart was hammering in her chest and she looked at him with a mixture of fascination and dismay.

'No.' Her voice was shaky and she shook her head. 'I can't do it.'

'Fine.' His tone was cold. 'Then your brother will be held accountable for the debt. Just how do you rate his chances of raising eight million pounds, Miss Kingston?'

Emily closed her eyes briefly.

Peter would *never* be able to get that sort of money. No wonder he'd vanished, she fretted, chewing her lip as she contemplated how her brother must be feeling. He'd probably gone into hiding, afraid to face the world. He must be worried sick.

If only he'd confided in her.

But he'd always seen himself in the role of her protector. He'd never really treated her as an adult. Probably didn't believe that she was capable of making an adult decision.

Emily swallowed.

Could she really turn her back on Peter now, having been given the chance to make things right?

Her gaze slid to the prince, who was watching her, the expression in his eyes veiled by thick, dark lashes.

'All right.' Her voice was a croak. 'My body seems to be my only asset so if you want it—'

He straightened and walked towards her, his dark eyes narrowed. 'I don't want a martyr in my bed,' he drawled lightly, 'so cease pretending that you don't burn for me the way I burn for you.'

She clenched her fingers into her palms, just *hating* herself for being so obvious and hating him even more for noticing. She really, really didn't want to question her decision too closely.

'You think you're just so irresistible,' she blurted out, mortification overruling discretion. 'You don't think there's a woman alive who would say no to you, do you?'

'Well, let's just say that I haven't met her yet,' he said dryly. 'But then being a wealthy prince does come with some advantages.'

He was suggesting that women threw themselves at him because of who he was. But she knew that for her the attraction had nothing to do with who he was and everything to do with what he was.

A wickedly attractive male.

Powerful, strong and totally in control of his surroundings.

And the female in her was drawn to him whether she liked it or not.

'All right. So—?' She looked at him expectantly, her whole body shivering with anticipation and he laughed.

'*So?* You think that I am going to throw you onto my Persian carpet and have my wicked way with you here and now?' His dark eyes gleamed. 'I have slightly more finesse than that, Emily. Anticipation is everything, don't you agree? The feast is altogether more satisfying when the hunger is intense.'

Anticipation was starting to make her stomach feel strange

and her whole body was wound so tightly that she could hardly breathe.

'So you'd rather wait—'

'When my ancestors wanted to assure privacy they returned to the desert.' His eyes glittered dark. 'I intend to do the same. Only this time I'll be taking you with me. As my wife.'

The desert?

Images exploded in her head and she remembered the wild loneliness of the landscape they'd driven through on the trip from the airport. A terrain as harsh and unforgiving as the prince himself.

She shivered, aware that he was still watching her.

He smiled. 'It will guarantee us privacy and for what I have in mind we most *definitely* need privacy.'

CHAPTER SEVEN

THREE days later, Emily stared up at Zak, unable to believe that they were now married.

Because his father was ill, they had all agreed on a quiet wedding but, even so, Emily had been startled by how quickly the ceremony had been arranged.

Everyone thought it was wonderfully romantic that the previously cynical, playboy prince had fallen so madly in love with a woman that he was determined to marry her as quickly as possible.

Only she and Zak knew the truth.

And now, finally, their vows had been exchanged and everyone was waiting for him to kiss her.

Aware that Zak's father was watching them with an expression of benign approval on his tired face, Emily was careful not to let any of her anxiety show.

She'd only met the ruler of Kazban a few days before but she'd warmed to him immediately and she had no desire to hurt him by allowing him to think that their marriage was anything but genuine.

So when Zak's dark head bent towards her she lifted her mouth willingly, telling herself that she was doing it for his father and her brother. That the kiss was part of the deal that they'd agreed.

She was completely unprepared for the immediate rush of heat that she felt when his mouth descended on hers. Compared to the previous kisses he'd given her, it was relatively restrained, but its impact was no less for that restraint.

Emily felt her whole body respond and, unable to stop herself, she leaned into him, seeking closer contact. His arm slid round her waist and he continued to kiss her until someone cleared their throat and Zak finally lifted his head, a strange expression glittering in his dark eyes as he stared down at her.

'My wife.' He said the words thoughtfully and she flushed slightly, assuming that there was at least a hint of mockery in those words.

After all, hadn't each of them entered the marriage for a reason that was far removed from love and romance?

She was dying to ask why he needed to get married at this particular time, when he'd avoided it for so long, but there was something about his arrogant, forbidding profile that made it impossible to voice the question.

She had no more time to dwell on his reasons because the wedding guests suddenly swarmed around them, eager to deliver congratulations. Emily had discovered that, although this had been billed as a 'small' wedding, Zak was part of a huge extended family and 'small' meant that she had to talk to an endless stream of well-wishers.

Grateful for his support, Emily wondered how he could be so convincing when both of them knew that this marriage was very much a business arrangement.

But he seemed determined to play the part of the attentive male, not leaving her side as they were approached by an endless stream of people whose names she had no hope of remembering.

Eventually they sat down at a long table to eat and, as she glanced round her, watching people as they talked and ate, she found herself wishing that Peter were there. He was the only family she had, after all, and she would have wanted him at her wedding even though it wasn't a wedding in the proper sense.

But it was because of Peter that this wedding was taking place.

'You are very quiet,' Zak said softly, his dark gaze raking her pale face. 'You are tired?'

'I was just wishing that Peter was here,' she said truthfully and his brows came together in a frown.

'Your brother has caused you much heartache,' he murmured, disapproval evident in the lines of his handsome face. 'Now that you are my wife, I will do everything I can to put that right.'

He sounded so caring that she actually had to remind herself that he'd married her simply because he needed a wife.

This wasn't real—

'You've married me and cancelled the debt,' she pointed out stiffly. 'I think you've done more than your share.'

Immediately after the wedding feast they left for the desert, delayed briefly by the reaction of Jamal who clung and cried and demanded not to be left.

'He is so little and he's had so much change,' Emily said softly to Zak as she cuddled the little boy. An army of palace staff had decorated the room in accordance with her instructions and it was bright and cheerful and full of light.

'You can't take Emily away!' Jamal glared at his uncle. 'I love Emily. Emily laughs and she cuddles and she's fun. And I like her stories.'

Zak swept the little boy into his arms. 'You discovered all that in such a short time? I will bring her back to you,' he promised, his voice surprisingly gentle as he reassured the child, 'but in the meantime I have found you a new nanny who you will love and who will also tell you great stories and—' he hesitated '—and I have arranged for your mama to come home.'

Still recovering from the shock of discovering that Zak was capable of real warmth, Emily noticed his mouth harden and wondered what it was about Jamal's mother that seemed to induce such tension in everyone.

Privately she was appalled that the woman seemed to show no interest in her own child and she was oddly touched that the prince seemed equally disapproving. He genuinely seemed to care for his little nephew and he had interviewed the new nanny personally. Fortunately the girl was very sweet and swiftly made friends with Jamal, who reluctantly agreed to let Emily go.

'But bring her back,' he ordered sulkily and his uncle's eyes gleamed.

'Be assured, I will bring her back.'

When I've finished with her, had been the unspoken message as he'd glanced at Emily and she'd coloured deeply.

And now they were one of a convoy of vehicles, all heading towards the oasis of Madan.

'I—I thought we'd be alone,' she ventured, glancing over her shoulder, and the prince gave a wry smile.

'"Alone" is a word that doesn't feature in my vocabulary,' he conceded, his hands tightening on the wheel as he held the vehicle steady on the difficult terrain. 'But when we reach the oasis we will most certainly be granted privacy. For what I have in mind I most certainly don't require any sort of audience.'

Emily turned her head away to hide her expression. The reference to their approaching wedding night made her *shrink* with embarrassment and as the Golden Palace of Kazban disappeared behind them she felt the tension rise.

She clung to the seat of the four-wheel drive vehicle, staring in fascination at the vast sand dunes that rose steeply in every direction. The sun played tricks with the colour, revealing browns, reds and rich golds.

'How on earth do you know where you're going?' She gazed at the sand dunes that stretched endlessly into the distance. 'I mean, it all looks the same.'

Maybe they'd get lost.

Maybe they'd have to return to the palace...

The prince glanced at her briefly. 'To a foreigner, maybe. To those familiar with the desert it is possible to navigate with only the wind and the stars as guides.'

'It's daylight,' Emily pointed out, her eyes narrowing

slightly, 'so there are no stars and we can't feel the wind thanks to air conditioned luxury.'

The prince smiled. 'I thought you preferred the more romantic slant,' he drawled lightly, 'but you are right, of course. And once we leave the road, I use a compass. It's built into the vehicle.'

A compass.

No chance of getting lost, then.

Emily slumped back in her seat, but against her will her eyes slid sideways and rested on the hard muscle of his thigh. For the journey he had discarded both suit and robes in favour of an old pair of black jeans and they fitted snugly, accentuating his athletic physique. Unable to help herself, she let her gaze flicker upwards slightly to where the fit of his trousers displayed the unmistakable evidence of his masculinity. Her stomach dropped and her mouth dried. No matter which conversation one of them started, the only words in her mind were *bed, bed, bed*.

How could he be so relaxed about the whole thing? she wondered helplessly, swiftly turning her head to hide the betraying colour in her cheeks. She was a complete bag of nerves and yet he was *totally* cool.

But then he probably made a habit of taking women into the desert to seduce them, she thought weakly, remembering her brother's comments about the prince's reputation with women. Shy and inexperienced he certainly wasn't!

Unlike her—

'We will be stopping at the stud farm first,' the prince told her, his sharp glance in the mirror reminding her that they were towing a horsebox behind them. For a moment she'd forgotten Sahara and the fact that the prince seemed to trust no one else with his precious stallion.

'We fly our other horses around,' he'd explained as he'd loaded the horse into the box himself, 'but Sahara hates flying and I won't subject him to the stress.'

His thoughtfulness on that score had surprised her. Maybe

she should turn herself into a horse, Emily mused. Then he might be more sympathetic.

Feeling gloomy again, she stared out of the window and her interest was caught by the changing scenery. The light played across the dunes, creating different patterns and eventually her eyes drifted closed.

When she awoke it was late afternoon and in the distance mountains loomed and she could see palm trees.

She frowned and smothered a yawn. 'What's that over there?'

'It's the oasis. We've arrived,' Zak told her and Emily's eyes widened.

'But it's huge! I thought an oasis would be small.'

'Sometimes they are and sometimes whole towns are built around an oasis,' he informed her, slowing his pace and suddenly changing direction. 'We will go first to the stud farm. I wish to see Sahara settled.'

Minutes later they were passing white painted fences and lush greenery. Emily blinked in astonishment at the contrast with the desert and then gave a gasp of delight as she saw horses, her tension momentarily forgotten.

'Arabs! Oh, they're beautiful—can we stop the car?' Emily already had her hand on the door and he obliged, bringing the vehicle to a halt. 'Look at the foals.' She jumped out of the vehicle and sprinted over to the white-painted fence. Her expression softened as she watched the two little foals. 'Aren't they gorgeous?'

'They are by Sahara,' came a voice from behind her and she turned to see that the prince had also climbed out of the four-wheel drive. 'Both fillies—and both with an impeccable bloodline. They will do well on the racetrack.'

Emily turned as she heard Sahara stamping impatiently in his box and calling to the mares.

Hearing the noise, the mares came galloping across the field to the fence, tails held high, nostrils flared in excitement and anticipation.

Despite her nerves, Emily gave Zak a rueful smile. 'Sahara knows he's home.'

'I think his emotions are slightly more basic than that,' he drawled slowly, his gaze slightly mocking as he looked down at her. 'He senses the mares and all of a sudden he has sex on the brain.'

Sex on the brain.

Suddenly Emily's eyes were trapped by his, her breathing compromised by the molten sexuality in those glittering black eyes. This must be how the mares were feeling, she thought breathlessly. Confronted by a powerful stallion with just one thing on his mind. Nervous and fascinated at the same time.

Zak stepped closer to her and suddenly she was overwhelmingly aware of his masculinity. As if her body had sensed his superior strength and mastery, she experienced a thrill of excitement that was totally alien to her.

'And the mares are equally excited,' he said in a soft drawl, gesturing towards the mares with a casual flick of his hand. 'Because the stallion is home.'

Warmth spread through her pelvis and Emily stood frozen to the spot, held still by the velvet seduction in his voice and the sheer power of his presence. Every female part of her reacted to the male in him and she felt herself sway towards him, drawn by the indefinable chemistry that seemed to connect them.

His eyes locked on hers and he gave a nod of pure masculine satisfaction. 'You will come to me tonight,' he said silkily, 'and it will be good.'

Emily was lost in those dark eyes. *You will come to me tonight.* She ought to slap his face for being so self assured and arrogant but instead she found herself wishing that she didn't have to wait until tonight.

She wanted him *now*.

Appalled by the direction of her thoughts, she backed away from him, reminding herself that she was doing this for Peter. She was cancelling the debt. It was a business deal—

So why was her body trembling with anticipation?

She shot him a look designed to freeze but he merely smiled, his expression infuriatingly enigmatic.

Confused and unsettled by her own feelings, she was relieved when a group of staff from the stud farm arrived to take Sahara.

The prince unboxed the horse himself and then turned him over to the head groom, issuing a string of instructions in Arabic.

The man nodded and led the horse away, leaving them alone.

'So where are we staying tonight, Your Highness?' She aimed at some degree of formality and the prince looked amused.

'We are married, *azîz*. I think we have reached the point in our relationship where you can call me Zak.'

'Our marriage was a business arrangement,' she reminded him stiffly. 'We don't have a relationship—'

'We will do by tonight,' he answered smoothly, his confidence absolute, 'and rest assured that I do not expect you to call me "Your Highness" when you are stretched out naked under me.'

Emily felt heat flood through her body at the vivid image his words created. 'You're trying to shock me.'

He lifted a hand and stroked her cheek, a curious expression on his handsome face as he ran a finger over her heated skin. 'I've never met a woman who blushes as often as you do.'

'I never blushed until I met you,' Emily muttered, feeling the maddeningly gentle touch of his fingers with every nerve of her body. 'Since I met you I'm the colour of a beetroot every minute of the day.'

He smiled. 'Because I'm so very shocking and you're so very innocent, Miss Kingston?'

There was no missing the irony in his tone and Emily bit her lip. This was her opportunity to try and tell him that he was totally wrong about her. But she couldn't bring herself to say the words.

'I'm doing this for my brother,' she croaked finally, and his smile broadened, his black eyes flickering down to her mouth.

'The ultimate sacrifice,' he murmured softly. 'In a few hours from now you will be lying on my bed, squirming and begging and I assure you, *azîz*, you will *not* be thinking of your brother.'

Emily pulled away from him feeling hot and strange and so furiously angry with him that she was ready to hit him!

Not daring to look back at him, she stalked back towards their vehicle and yanked open the door, vowing that whatever happened between them she most certainly wouldn't squirm *or* beg.

She was going to lie there with her eyes shut and her mouth shut and his incredible ego was going to have to survive without any help from her!

She scrambled into her seat and moments later he joined her, springing into the driver's seat with athletic grace and driving his foot down on the accelerator.

Without Sahara to consider he drove swiftly, sparing not a thought for the others trying to follow.

In a relatively short time they reached the other side of the oasis and Emily saw a series of enormous tents.

Well, they weren't exactly tents, she conceded, staring in awe at the vast expanse of canvas that stretched before her. The prince obviously needed space when he was away from home.

'The desert can be dangerous,' the prince warned, leaning across and releasing her seat belt, 'so you would be wise not to wander far while you are out here, *azîz*.'

She glared at him, still angered by his own total self-assurance. Didn't he feel even the slightest glimmer of nerves about the forthcoming night? But then why would he? she reasoned gloomily. He was an experienced, sophisticated man of the world whereas she—

'What could possibly be more dangerous than you?'

His sinfully sexy mouth curved into a smile. 'Well, I would have said snakes and scorpions, but it's for you to decide, my beautiful English rose.'

Snakes and scorpions?

Emily looked at him in dismay and opened the door gingerly, staring down at the ground with trepidation.

The prince reached a hand inside a pocket of the vehicle and removed a dagger. 'Perhaps you would feel safer with this,' he mocked gently as he handed it to her. 'Then you can defend yourself against intruders. Eight-legged or otherwise. Providing you don't wander into the desert unaccompanied you should be perfectly safe.'

She took the dagger, noting the beautiful carving on the handle. 'Thanks.' Having examined it closely, she handed it back. 'You'd better keep it. I'm not that great with violence.'

'Ah, yes.' He took the dagger and dealt her a sizzling smile. 'I remember now—the princess and the water pistol.'

His smile held so much charisma that her stomach felt hollow and her legs wobbled.

Furious with herself for falling so easily for his charm, she dragged her gaze away from his mouth and swallowed hard.

She was not going to squirm or beg, she reminded herself firmly.

Suddenly realizing that an army of staff was waiting to greet them, she slid out of the vehicle, lifting a hand to her hair, conscious that she'd been travelling all day. She must look a total mess. She would have given anything for a long soak in a bath but doubtless such luxuries were unavailable out in the desert.

She was surprised and pleased when Aisha stepped forward. She hadn't even realized that she was part of the group who was travelling with them. 'If you would follow me, Your Highness. You must be tired after the journey.'

Your Highness?

Suddenly realizing that there was more to marrying a prince than legalized sex, Emily hurried after her, not casting a backward glance at the prince. 'Call me Emily, Aisha.'

The girl looked shocked. 'That would not be proper, Your Highness. You are a princess now and tonight we will make you so beautiful for the Prince.'

Emily's sharp declaration that she'd rather go in jeans, just to make a point, froze on her lips when she saw the beautiful dresses hanging up ready for her to select one.

'Oh.' She stepped up to the rail and touched the first one, a shimmering blue silk that changed colour with the light.

'I love that one too,' Aisha agreed, her tone excited as she took the dress down and held it against Emily. 'It will look wonderful. But first you must have a bath.'

'Where?' Emily glanced round the 'room' for the first time and her mouth fell open.

It was like something straight out of the Arabian nights. The flaps of the tent had been drawn back, affording a breathtaking view of the desert, and the whole room was colourful and mysterious. Decorated in deep reds and purples, the floor was covered in Persian rugs so beautiful that Emily caught her breath.

There was a noise from outside the door and four more female servants entered, bowing and smiling and carrying hot water. 'The prince has asked us to help you dress for dinner, my lady.'

Emily stood still while Aisha unzipped her dress and chatted happily. 'But how you are fortunate! To have fallen in love with the prince and for him to fall in love with you—it is *so* romantic.'

Romantic?

Emily bit her lip, unwilling to disillusion the girl. She knew exactly why the prince had married her and his reasons were far from romantic. He needed a wife and, for some reason, he'd chosen her. He was behaving like his stallion. *He had sex on the brain.*

'All right, Aisha.' She tipped her head on one side and looked at the bath. 'Let's get on with this.'

Two hours later, she stared at her reflection in awe. Instead of allowing her to sleep after her bath, Aisha had urged her to sit in the chair where she'd done her hair and makeup and then helped her to dress.

Her newly washed hair flowed down her back and glinted with the tiny flecks of gold thread that Aisha had cleverly woven into the strands and her eyes had been outlined with kohl and they suddenly seemed enormous.

And the dress was *amazing*. She'd never worn anything so beautiful in her life.

She turned sideways to look at herself in the mirror, hardly recognizing herself. It looked Eastern and exotic, skimming her figure lightly, hinting and suggesting at what lay underneath without being blatantly provocative. And yet at the same time it felt incredibly sensual against her skin.

How had he guessed her size so accurately? A flush spread across her body as she acknowledged the likelihood that the prince was well acquainted with female sizes.

Aisha had gasped in delight as she'd slipped the dress over Emily's head.

'Oh!' She'd covered her mouth with her hand. 'That shade of blue really suits you. You look every inch a princess.'

'Let's not get carried away here,' Emily muttered dryly, pushing aside the romantic thoughts that had been with her since childhood. There was going to be nothing romantic about tonight, she thought. The man might be spectacularly good-looking, but he was also cold and ruthless, and tonight was certainly not about romance. It was all about sex.

So why was her stomach full of butterflies and why was her pulse racing in frantic anticipation?

'How long have we got, Aisha?'

'His Highness has requested that you join him as soon as you are ready,' the other girl said quickly and Emily took a deep breath, feeling as though she'd never be ready.

'Well, let's go, then.' Before she bolted into the desert and took her chances with the snakes and the scorpions.

Aisha pulled back the flap on the tent and Emily was surprised to see Sharif standing there. Her cheeks flamed. Was the entire staff of the palace present to witness her first night with the prince?

He gave a bow. 'I have come to escort you to dinner,' he said gravely and she gave Aisha a warm smile.

'Thanks for everything.'

'Have a wonderful evening, Your Highness.' Aisha's eyes were wide with awe and Emily reflected that to some, marrying the prince was obviously considered on a par with winning the lottery.

She walked up to Sharif with a smile. 'Ready when you are.'

His gaze slid over her, starting with her golden hair and finishing with the blue silk slippers that adorned her feet and matched the fabric in her dress. Then he gave a faint sigh.

'It was inevitable,' he murmured to himself and gestured for her to follow him down the canopied corridor.

Wondering exactly what was inevitable, Emily hurried after him, but there was no opportunity to ask because almost immediately Sharif entered another tent and bowed low.

The prince strode forward and Sharif immediately melted away, leaving the two of them alone.

Suffering from a sudden attack of nerves, Emily stood still and wondered if the time would come when she would be able to look at him and not shake with longing. He really was *indecently* good-looking, she thought helplessly, her eyes running over his broad shoulders and resting on the tantalizing cluster of dark hair visible at the throat of his open-neck shirt. He'd changed into a pair of beautifully tailored trousers but, despite his outward appearance of

Western sophistication, he still managed to look exotic and dangerous. His eyes glittered dark as he studied her, his legs spread wide in a stance of supreme self-confidence.

His eyes slid over her with a gratifying amount of male appreciation. 'You look beautiful.'

Hideously self-conscious and not knowing exactly what was expected of her, she gave a little shrug and glanced down at herself. 'You chose it.'

'I wasn't talking about the dress.'

Her cheeks coloured under his burning scrutiny and she'd never felt more awkward in her life. They both knew that this wasn't exactly an ordinary courtship and she certainly hadn't expected compliments. What happened now? Did they eat? Talk? *Or did they—*

'You're shaking.'

'Well, I'm nervous,' she confessed, fiddling with her hands and then wrapping her arms around her middle. 'It's not every day a girl joins a harem.'

'I married you, *azîz*. So no harem.' He gave a predatory smile, as relaxed as she was tense. 'This is an exclusive arrangement. Just you and me and an *extremely* large bed.'

Her eyes slid to the bed and she felt her cheeks heat and her legs weaken alarmingly. Draped in rich coloured silks, it dominated the room, inviting the occupant to recline on its vastness, to sink into the soft, satiny cushions and to lose herself in female fantasy.

Emily felt her body warm.

The prince certainly knew how to play to a woman's fantasies, she thought weakly, a strange feeling that she didn't recognize curling deep in the pit of her stomach. She stared at the bed and had a fleeting and decidedly unsettling image of herself lying on those silk sheets, entwined with a man—but not just any man. A man with eyes as dark as night and a man with a heritage that began in the desert.

A man who could kiss a woman into a stupor.

Appalled by the uncharacteristically sexual nature of her

thoughts, Emily dragged her eyes away, reminding herself that she wasn't exactly qualified to do justice to the bed.

Aware that the prince was looking at her with a lazy, slumberous gaze, she felt her heart rate increase at an alarming rate.

'I can see you're expecting a lot.'

'This display of feminine shyness is totally wasted on me,' he drawled softly, strolling around her slowly. 'We are both adults and we both want the same thing.'

Did they?

She wasn't at all sure what she wanted.

She'd thought that she just wanted to go home, but suddenly the only thing in her head was *him*.

And the bed—

When she still didn't answer, he gave a shrug, his eyes amused. 'Let me spell it out more clearly. If you wish to play elaborate games then, of course, I shall oblige, but it is entirely unnecessary. You are a modern young woman, not an innocent virgin, and I'm perfectly comfortable with that.'

Emily wondered just how comfortable he'd feel if he knew that she'd never done any more than kiss a man before.

Eyeing the enormous bed once more she suddenly felt ridiculously nervous and decided that she *had* to tell him the truth. She just wasn't any good at lying and surely the minute he stripped her naked, he'd *know*.

'I—er—we need to have a talk, Your Highness,' she began, and he strolled towards her, his black eyes raking her tense face.

'Zak.'

She sucked in a breath. 'Zak—I know you think that I— well, you're completely wrong about me and I think you ought to know that I haven't—well—' She broke off, scarlet with mortification. 'I've never—' She broke off again, letting the words hang, hoping that he'd got the message.

His gaze rested on hers, a mixture of exasperation and amusement lighting his dark eyes. 'Fine.' His broad shoulders lifted in a dismissive shrug. 'Then I look forward to introducing you to the joys of sex.'

CHAPTER EIGHT

SHE couldn't move, couldn't breathe, her whole body singed by the blatantly sexual nature of Zak's words and his gaze.

The joys of sex.

She'd expected him to be at least slightly fazed by the discovery that she was a virgin, but he didn't seem remotely bothered.

He'd accepted it without as much of a blink of those inky dark lashes.

The reality of the situation suddenly loomed large and her tummy tumbled.

It was actually going to happen.

Nerves fluttered frantically in her stomach, mingling with a deep, throbbing ache that began in her pelvis and spread slowly through her body. All those years she'd dreamed about what it would be like and now she was about to find out.

'Are you hungry?' Zak gestured to the low table that was spread with a variety of tempting dishes and Emily placed a hand on her churning stomach.

Hungry?

She was far too nervous to eat a thing, but if she refused then she knew what the alternative entertainment would be—

Suddenly needing to postpone the moment for as long as possible, she managed a smile.

'Starving,' she lied, walking over to the cushions and seating herself comfortably.

To her dismay, Zak seated himself right next to her, his muscular thigh brushing hers as he sat down, leaving her breathlessly aware of his masculinity.

Feeling positively weak at the knees, she was relieved that she was already sitting. She didn't know how she was going to eat anything. Her stomach was churning and so full of butterflies that there was *definitely* no room for anything else.

'Wine?'

He poured her a glass and handed it to her and she took it eagerly and took several large gulps, hoping that it would make her relax.

But relaxing was impossible. How could she relax when he was lounging so close to her and she was aware of every male inch of him? She put her goblet down, her hand shaking so much that she was afraid she might spill the wine.

'Tell me about your family.' He spooned some food onto her plate and she immediately stiffened, her whole manner defensive.

'If you're trying to trap me into saying something about Peter—'

'Relax.' He gave the order softly, his eyes amused as they raked her tense features. 'Tonight we are *not* at war with each other. My question was an innocent one—I merely wished to discover more about you. We are, after all, married.'

But the marriage wasn't real—

She stared at him. 'Peter *is* my family,' she said flatly, taking another large gulp of the wine. It really was completely delicious and, although she never usually drank, she rapidly decided that the only way she was ever going to get through this evening was if she had something to relax her. 'He's all I have in the world.'

The prince's eyes narrowed and his gaze was speculative. 'All you have? How so?'

'Our parents died when I was twelve.' Emily looked at him, wondering why he was suddenly so interested in her. 'I went to live with Peter.'

'He is much older than you?'

'Fifteen years.' Emily gave a bleak smile. 'I suppose I was an afterthought. Anyway, Peter and his wife took me in.'

He frowned. 'They had no children of their own?'

Emily shook her head and concentrated on pushing her food around her plate.

'Paloma never wanted children.'

'But she had you.'

'Not through choice.' Emily picked up her wine again, not wanting to reveal such an intimate part of herself to him. She didn't want him to know just how much she longed to be part of a real family. Peter had done his best to make her feel wanted, but nothing had been able to disguise his wife's irritation at being landed with a child she hadn't wanted.

And lying in her bedroom alone, trying to fill the bone-deep loneliness night after night, Emily had lost herself in books and stories of happy families and she'd vowed that one day that would be her.

She didn't need a prince and she didn't need a palace, but what she did need was love.

Which was ironic, really, she reflected, reaching dizzily for her wine, because she seemed to have ended up with the prince and the palace but not the love.

Deciding that life certainly had a way of surprising you, she was about to take another mouthful when the glass was gently removed from her hand.

'I think this evening would be more exciting for both of us if you weren't unconscious,' he drawled, spooning a selection of food onto her plate. 'Try this. It's a local speciality.'

Having thought that she wouldn't be able to eat a thing, Emily suddenly discovered that the food was delicious and she nibbled a few pieces before stopping and looking at him.

'What about you? It must have been pretty lonely being a prince.'

His eyes met hers above his wineglass. 'I have been surrounded by people since I was born. To be lonely is a fantasy.'

Emily thought about that and then nodded. 'I can see that it must be difficult to get time on your own, but you can be surrounded by people and still be lonely. Especially if you suspect their motives. But at least you had family who you could trust.'

His shoulders tensed visibly. 'Do you always have such a naïve approach to life?'

She looked at him warily, unsure what she'd said to engender the bitterness she detected. 'I just mean that families usually stick together—'

'Do they? Is that another one of your fantasies?' His gaze was enigmatic and Emily bit her lip, not knowing how to respond. She was used to dealing with very young children who hadn't had time to be damaged by life. A cynical adult was outside her scope of experience.

She turned the question back on him. 'Don't you think that families should be able to rely on each other?'

Zak drained his glass of wine. 'I think it is foolish to ever rely on another person.' His face was suddenly cold and unsmiling and she wondered what had happened to make him so suspicious of everyone. To make him so ruthlessly independent that he'd even dismiss his own family.

'So why haven't you married before now?' She asked the question without thinking and his features froze. Sensing that she'd said the wrong thing, Emily was about to apologize when he gave a slight smile.

'The time wasn't right, *azîz*.'

Sensing that he was holding something back, she was dying to question him further but something in his cool gaze prevented her from speaking.

Feeling decidedly woozy and wishing that she hadn't drunk the wine quite so quickly on an empty stomach, Emily slipped off her shoes and snuggled back on the cushions.

'This is an amazing tent. *So* comfortable,' she murmured,

gazing around her. 'I've always thought I'd hate camping, but you certainly know how to do it in style.'

Zak smiled and followed her gaze. 'You had visions of pegging down tent poles in the desert?'

'Something like that. Is it here all the time?'

Zak nodded. 'It is my home when I am visiting the stud farm or sorting out problems among the tribe. They come and see me here. It is a simple life. Less complicated than living in the palace at Kazban.'

Emily eyed the bed again and decided that it didn't look that simple. And, remembering the entourage of staff who had accompanied them through the desert, she questioned the prince's definition of privacy.

'Does your father come here too?'

'As you have observed, my father no longer enjoys good health,' Zak replied evenly, 'and he prefers to remain in the palace with Jamal.'

Emily smiled. 'Your little nephew is gorgeous.'

'You like children—' A strange expression crossed his face and she looked at him in surprise.

'I love children. Why wouldn't I?'

'Because not all women do,' he replied carefully and Emily frowned.

'Well, I suppose that's true.' After all, Paloma definitely didn't love children. 'But I do. Especially Jamal's age.' She snuggled into the cushions, smiling to herself. 'I love the way they're so excited about everything. And they just learn *so* fast. One minute they're recognizing letters and then the next minute they're stringing them together and they're reading and that is just the *best* thing. Seeing a child spell a word out for the first time just makes me smile and smile.'

A long silence greeted that declaration and she blushed. 'Sorry. I was chatting too much. I always do that when I'm nervous.'

Night-black eyes meshed with hers. 'Why would you be nervous?'

Her smile faltered. Was he seriously asking her that? She'd already told him that she'd never done this before.

'I'm afraid of getting lost in the bed,' she joked feebly and he gave a soft laugh.

'I can assure you that there is no chance of that, *habibati*.'

Emily felt the tension rise to such heights that every nerve ending in her body was screaming. Her eyes dropped to his gorgeous mouth and she had to clench her fists to stop herself reaching for him and dragging his head down to hers.

Why didn't he kiss her?

Hadn't he invited her into the desert for the express purpose of seducing her?

And yet so far he hadn't laid a finger on her.

Her whole body was so agonizingly aware of him that she thought she'd melt with longing.

But still he didn't make a move towards her.

Perhaps he'd changed his mind.

But then she tumbled headlong into his smouldering black gaze and knew that he hadn't changed his mind.

He was playing games with her.

'So, Emily…' His eyes glittered as he looked at her and she looked back at him dizzily, her heart beating faster as she gazed into his wicked black eyes. He was so impossibly handsome she just wanted to stare and stare.

And touch—

His mouth drifted closer to hers. 'So, Emily, tell me your wildest fantasies.'

Her wildest fantasies?

At the moment they all involved him and the bed that was waiting for them in the corner. But the detail was vague. She didn't have enough experience to know exactly what she wanted him to do, but she knew she wanted him to do *something*, and *quickly*, before her body melted with longing—

She stared up at him, just *willing* him to kiss her, but instead he rose to his feet and swept her up in his arms before striding across the room with her. He lowered her gently to the floor next to the bed and then placed his hands on her shoulders.

Shaking with anticipation, Emily lifted her eyes to his and caught her breath as she saw the heat and purpose in his shimmering black gaze.

His mouth came down on hers with seductive gentleness, in complete contrast to the madness of their previous kisses. This time his kiss was leisurely, almost teasing, and she lifted her hands and placed them on his chest. Her fingers curled into hard muscle, feeling the slow thud of his heartbeat and the tantalizing warmth of his skin through the thin silk of his shirt.

She felt the erotic slide of his tongue against her lips and her mouth opened under his, her heart thumping hard as he encouraged her to allow a more intimate exploration

As he deepened the kiss a slow burn of heat flared deep in her pelvis and grew and grew until her whole body was on fire with longing.

And still he kissed her, his long fingers sliding down her bare arms as he explored her mouth with explicit strokes of his tongue.

The heat grew inside her and she felt his hands move across her back and then suddenly her dress slid from her shoulders and pooled at her feet leaving her dressed only in her underwear.

Emily gasped against his mouth, but before she could speak he scooped her up in his arms, lowered her into the centre of the bed and came down on top of her.

She felt his weight holding her still and then his mouth came down on hers again, his kiss hot and hard as his hand slid over her heated skin and cupped one full breast.

He removed her bra without her ever knowing how and then finally lifted his head, his eyes glittering black as he stared down at her.

'Without doubt you were designed for a man's pleasure,'

he said huskily, lowering his head once more, this time to claim the rosy jut of her nipple with his mouth.

At the first skilled flick of his tongue, she arched and cried out, shocked by the intensity of the feelings that exploded inside her, but he held her down with the weight of his powerful body, keeping her captive as his mouth created magic.

'Zak—' She gasped his name and writhed underneath him, driven wild by the intolerable heat in her pelvis.

He lifted his head, his breathing unsteady as his hand slid slowly down her body, lingered for a brief moment on her hip and then rested on the most private place of all.

Emily held her breath. Her cheeks burned and part of her felt shy and self-conscious but another part of her wanted him to touch her so badly that she didn't *care*.

She almost sobbed with relief as his fingers eased inside her silk panties and then gasped as he parted her and sought access to the very heart of her.

It was the most intimate experience of her life and her cheeks flamed as she felt him explore her, each expert stroke of his fingers releasing a flood of sensation that swamped her excited, shivering body.

Emily was on fire.

Her body wanted something more. Desire pulsed through her and she reached up and grabbed the front of his shirt, wanting to feel his skin against hers.

Her fingers shook as she fumbled with the buttons and all the time he continued to take shocking liberties with her body, his dark eyes slumberous and wickedly sexy as he watched her squirming beneath him.

'You like that.' Blatantly smug at the havoc he was creating in her body, he allowed her to remove his shirt and closed his eyes as she slid her hands over his hair-roughened torso.

Dark hair shadowed the powerful muscle of his chest and

she touched him with awe, acutely aware of his male strength.

Feverish with need, she moved her hands to the waistband of his trousers and she fumbled with his zip, desperation making her clumsy.

Dealing her an all-male smile, he placed his hand on hers and helped her finish the task, discarding the rest of his clothes with an impatient movement before coming back on top of her.

Suddenly she felt impossibly shy, her cheeks flaming at her first brief glimpse of an aroused male. Shocked blue eyes met amused black.

'You are allowed to look, *habibati*,' he drawled softly, lowering his head and kissing her briefly on the mouth. 'And you may also touch.'

Touch—

Her heart pattering ridiculously fast, she slid her hand down his body and then hesitated, afraid of doing the wrong thing. Of touching him in the wrong way.

And then she felt his hand cover hers and draw it downwards until her fingers stroked along the length of his pulsing shaft. The discovery that she couldn't quite circle him with her hand made her stomach shift with nerves. But surely the female body was designed to accommodate even the most powerful male, she assured herself, closing her eyes as she felt his silken hardness and heard his harsh groan.

'Enough—' With a decisive movement he pulled away from her gentle caress and came down on top of her, settling himself between her thighs.

She felt the throb of his erection touching her intimately and instinctively arched closer to him, her whole body humming with a sexual excitement so intense that it threatened to overwhelm her.

He paused and she shifted impatiently beneath him, needing him to relieve the intolerable ache that was consuming her entire body.

He raked the tangled blonde hair away from her flushed face with a far from steady hand and then slid an arm under her hips, lifting her slightly.

She felt his bold shaft stretching her and then he thrust deep, sheathing himself inside her in a powerful movement. Emily gave a shocked cry of pain and dug her nails in his back in an instinctive attempt to stop him moving.

His body stilled immediately and his hand cupped her chin, forcing her to meet his incredulous gaze.

'Emily?' His husky question required an answer, but she could give him none because she was afraid to breathe, afraid to move in case the pain returned. And anyway, she didn't understand his shocked reaction. She'd *told* him that she was a virgin—

But for some reason there was a tension about him that hadn't been there before and he hesitated before lowering his mouth to hers and kissing her gently, the erotic probe of his tongue stoking the fire again.

'Relax and I swear I will not hurt you again.' He muttered the words against her mouth and then gave a groan of apology, 'It hurt only because I didn't know—'

Her hands were still clutching the smooth skin of his shoulders, willing him not to move. 'But I told you—'

His breathing was unsteady. 'And I did not believe you. And that shames me.'

'Doesn't matter,' Emily breathed, suddenly conscious that the pain had gone and a very different sensation was building inside her. She moved her hips experimentally and he drew in a ragged breath.

'We should stop—'

'No!' Not recognizing what was happening to her own body, Emily slid her arms around his neck. 'No, don't stop. Please.'

He stared down into her face for endless seconds and then he lowered his mouth to hers and kissed her gently. 'I will be very gentle,' he promised huskily, 'and you will tell me if I hurt you again.'

Her heart thudding uncomfortably, Emily moved her hips again and he gave a low laugh.

'You were built for pleasure, *azîz*, and it will be my fortune to show you just how great that pleasure can be.'

He looked dark and masculine above her and she sucked in a breath sharply as he altered her position and withdrew slightly before thrusting again, his eyes on her face as he moved.

The feel of him against her and inside her was so exquisite that she cried out and slid her hands over his silken back, this time urging him on.

'Slowly, *azîz*,' he cautioned softly. 'I will not hurt you a second time.'

'You're not hurting me,' she gasped, 'but, Zak, I need— *please*—'

But he refused to quicken the pace, instead taking her with agonizing slowness, each thrust a sensual torment as he taught her body the true meaning of desire.

And she felt the pressure in her body build and build until she was sobbing and gasping against his mouth, desperate for the fulfilment that eluded her.

'You are *mine*, *azîz*, only mine.' he uttered the words against her mouth and then thrust deep and hard, his lovemaking suddenly fierce and possessive. He was all heat and power, controlling her response until she finally reached a climax so intense that she cried out his name again and again, her fingers biting into his back as she felt him shudder against her.

Emily felt tears choke her and closed her eyes tightly, determined not to show him the level of emotion he'd induced.

She just hadn't known—

Hadn't imagined that it could ever be like that.

Not just the excitement but the amazing closeness. His

lovemaking had somehow driven out the loneliness that had
been part of her for so long. For the first time in her life
she'd felt a perfect connection with another human being.

She held tight to his body, loving the feel of his weight
on her, not wanting the moment to end.

But inevitably it did and Zak rolled onto his back, taking
her with him, his arms holding her firmly against him. 'That
was amazing.'

Too shy to look at him, she snuggled closer and pressed
a kiss to his damp skin, her body throbbing.

He didn't answer and when she risked a look at him she
saw that his eyes were closed, thick dark lashes brushing his
high cheekbones.

Emily bit her lip and snuggled back down beside him,
feeling disappointed and more than a little confused. Surely
it was customary for the man to say *something*.

Unless there was nothing to say.

Obviously it had been less than amazing for him, she concluded miserably. She'd disappointed him. So now what
happened?

She'd been a virgin.

Zak lay still until he felt her fall asleep and then he gently
disengaged himself from her arms, sprang out of bed and
reached for his trousers.

Grim-faced and tense, he jerked them on, satisfied himself
that she still slept and then pulled aside the flap of the tent
and strode out into the darkness, needing fresh air and space
to gather his thoughts.

Ignoring the guards on duty, he stared up at the night sky
and wondered exactly when he'd become so cynical that he
was no longer able to believe in the existence of innocence.
At what point of his life had he ceased to trust anything that
anyone said to him?

He ran a hand over his face and his body throbbed with
tension as he recalled the number of times she'd tried to tell

him, and the number of times he'd dismissed her nervousness as merely part of an elaborate act on her part.

Shifting uncomfortably under the unfamiliar weight of guilt, he searched for ways of justifying his behaviour. Was the blame really all his? After all, he would *not* have expected a virgin to agree to his proposition with the readiness that she had. Which surely just proved that her morals were every bit as dubious as he'd first suspected.

The question of *why* she was still a virgin troubled him slightly, but he decided grimly that it was obviously because she'd never needed to make the ultimate sacrifice before. It appalled him that she valued herself so lightly.

But then Emily Kingston was obviously willing to do whatever it took to avoid the debt.

First she'd tried to escape and when that hadn't worked she'd tried the usual feminine emotional blackmail—tears and fainting—and when that still left him unmoved she'd turned to the oldest female trick of all. Seduction.

Hadn't she been casting hot looks in his direction since that first day when she'd walked into his palace?

Hadn't this been *exactly* what she'd wanted all along?

Satisfied that he was absolved of blame, he strode purposefully back into the tent, intending to demand a further conversation with her.

But one glance at the bed stopped him dead.

She was lying across the bed fast asleep, her amazing blonde hair spread wildly across his pillow, her body covered by a silken throw. Her cheeks were flushed and she was smiling slightly in her sleep.

Zak felt something tighten inside him.

She looked incredibly young and innocent, but of course she wasn't any more.

He'd taken that innocence.

Intense sexual desire slammed through him at the memory.

Battling against the urge to wake her so that he could once

more experience innocence and teach her all the things she had yet to learn, he decided that he needed a very long, very cold shower before he could even begin to consider conversing with her.

He was about to turn when she opened her eyes and saw him.

Zak tensed but she merely stretched out a hand in invitation and smiled a womanly smile.

'Why are you dressed?' Her voice was husky with sleep. 'Come back to bed.'

He didn't move, held still by indecision, knowing that he should leave but unable to break the connection between them. 'In the circumstances I don't think that's a good idea.'

'What circumstances?' She struggled to sit up, confusion showing on her features. Zak gritted his teeth and reminded himself that Emily Kingston might have been innocent in the physical sense but it ended there.

Psychologically she'd been born with a woman's skill and need to manipulate.

She was still clutching the silk throw, her expression uncertain.

'If this is about the fact that I hadn't done it before—'

His jaw tightened. 'I was surprised.'

She looked at him. 'Well, I can't see why,' she said shyly. 'I told you enough times.'

But he hadn't believed her. When had a woman ever told him the truth before?

Her expression was anxious. 'I did everything wrong, didn't I? That's why you suddenly stalked out of the bed.'

He saw her fingers clutch the sheet and her smile falter and his jaw clenched hard. Consoling himself with the fact that if she wanted to offer herself so freely, then it would be wrong of him to reject her, he strolled up to the bed and sat down next to her.

'I did *not* stalk,' he said tightly. 'I needed fresh air.'

And a clear head.

She blushed slightly and he tensed as her eyes dropped to his mouth. She kept doing that and every time she did it he just wanted to flatten her beneath him and kiss her until she couldn't speak.

'I was pretty nervous,' she confessed shyly, 'but it was fantastic. Are you cross with me?'

The silk throw slipped and he was treated to a tantalizing glimpse of the shadowy dip between her full breasts.

She was completely and utterly gorgeous and she was lying in *his* bed, eyes huge and hopeful.

'Definitely not cross,' he assured her, removing his trousers and joining her under the silk throw in a decisive movement.

After all, they'd already done it *once*—

With a sigh of pleasure she wrapped her arms and legs around him and he brought his mouth down on hers with masculine purpose. His hand locked in her blonde hair, its softness teasing his senses and sending his already rampant libido into overdrive.

Her hands slid down his body, confident this time, and he groaned as he felt her touch him intimately, her fingers stroking him until he thought he'd explode.

With a rough curse he rolled on his back and took her with him, lifting her in an easy movement so that she straddled him.

Her cheeks were flushed and her eyes were hazy with desire and he positioned her carefully, holding back, determined not to hurt her a second time.

But this time she took the initiative, moving boldly until they were joined, her eyes widening as she took him deep inside her.

His gaze held by the look in her wide eyes, Zak tried to remember a time when sex had *ever* felt like this before. He failed.

It was just because she'd been a virgin, he assured himself, his jaw tightening as he struggled to detach his mind and *not* respond like an overexcited teenager.

It was because everything she was learning, she was learning from him.

Determined to hang onto his self-control, he closed his eyes and grasped her hips firmly, attempting to slow her movements, but she gave a whimper of protest and moved faster, circling her hips and generating a rhythm that drove them both towards an explosive climax.

She collapsed onto him and he wrapped his arms around her, his grip fierce as he held her close.

As he struggled to regain the control for which he prided himself it occurred to him that things were *not* going the way he'd planned them.

CHAPTER NINE

ZAK was gone.

Emily sat up sharply and glanced round the tent, her heart sinking as she realized that there was no sight of him.

If she needed any further confirmation that last night had been a disaster for him, then she had it now.

Remembering everything that had happened and just how uninhibited she'd been, she sank back against the pillows with an embarrassed groan.

Squirming and begging. Wasn't that what he had promised and hadn't she just rolled over and done exactly as he'd predicted?

Mortified by her own lack of cool, Emily rolled over and buried her face in the pillow with a groan.

And if once wasn't enough she'd summoned him back to bed so that he could make her squirm and beg for a second and third time.

And if she knew anything about Zak then they were going to have to look for another tent because there was no way this one would be big enough for the two of them and his ego after her performance last night.

Looking back on it, it was perfectly obvious that he regretted what they'd done, that he hadn't enjoyed it—why else would he have left the tent? But she'd been so brazen that she'd all but dragged him back into bed, leaving him absolutely no choice but to make love to her a second time.

No wonder he was always claiming that women threw themselves at him. She'd thrown herself so hard that she'd virtually *flattened* him.

She sat upright, her face hot with embarrassment. How was she supposed to face him after *that*?

And somehow she had to retain her dignity for just long enough for him to return her to the palace.

Judging from his reaction the night before, he obviously didn't consider her a reasonable exchange for her brother's debt. He was probably regretting the fact that he'd ever married her.

Her body ached all over and she would have dearly loved a bath but she was far too embarrassed by what had happened to even *think* about leaving his tent. After all, everyone knew why he'd brought her here so presumably everyone knew what they'd been doing all night and that knowledge just made her want to bury herself under the silk throw and never see the light of day again.

She was just wondering how she was going to discreetly disappear from his bed when the entrance of the tent was jerked to one side and he strode in, fully clothed and obviously fresh from the shower.

His dark hair was damp and slicked back from his brow and his jaw was freshly shaven and he looked so incredibly handsome that she felt her stomach tumble over and over.

Not knowing what to say, she pulled the covers up to her chin and watched him warily.

'You ate nothing last night—you must be hungry.' He snapped his fingers and an army of servants hurried in carrying various dishes and pots that they placed on the table that had been miraculously cleared from the night before.

Emily stared in astonishment. They must have come in while she'd slept—

Her embarrassment deepened and she vowed that if she ever wriggled herself out from this agonizing situation, she was *never* sleeping with a man again.

The servants prepared the table once more and then melted from the room discreetly, bowing low as they did so.

The prince strolled over to the bed and handed her a robe. 'You might find this more comfortable than your blue dress.'

'Thanks.' She snatched it from him with one hand, still

clutching the covers with the other. The memories of how she'd crawled all over him the night before still loomed large in her head and she avoided his gaze, determined not to show him how badly he affected her.

If he could be cool, then so could she.

Somehow she managed to wriggle into the robe without revealing a single inch of herself and she swung her legs onto the floor, gritting her teeth to prevent herself from uttering the whimper of pain that lodged in her throat as she discovered that her body ached in any number of unexpected places.

Brooding dark eyes fixed on her searchingly and she smiled blandly, rising to her feet in a smooth movement and contriving to walk normally across to the table.

'The coffee smells good.'

'We know how to make coffee.' He lounged next to her and her eyes rested on his strong forearms.

He knew how to make love too.

'I wish to talk to you about last night.' He said the words stiffly and she stilled in dismay.

She, on the other hand, had absolutely no desire to talk about last night. She did *not* need reminding that she'd produced the exact reaction that he'd predicted. Or that he'd been horrified to discover that she'd been a virgin.

'Those look delicious.' Hoping to divert him, she pointed to a plate of tiny pastries, and he handed them over, his eyes fixed on her face.

'We have much to talk about.'

Deciding that if he were determined to talk then they'd better get it over with, she bit into a pastry and gave a careless shrug. 'What's to talk about? You scored. End of story.'

There was a shocked silence and incredulous dark eyes raked hers. 'I *scored*?'

'Yes.' She took another bite of pastry. 'Isn't that what this is all about? Male supremacy? You wanted to prove that you could make me squirm and beg and I did just that. Congratulations. Another notch on your bedpost.'

His jaw hardened and he seemed unusually tense. 'That is *not* what happened last night.'

'No?' She put the pastry back on the plate, her appetite gone. 'Don't think that I didn't notice that you spent the whole night trying to escape from the tent. *Not* particularly flattering, I might add.'

He sucked in a breath. 'Until last night I was not aware that you were a virgin,' he said tightly and she shrugged.

'Well, it's hardly my fault if you're a born cynic,' she returned blithely, ignoring the bumping of her heart against her chest. 'And having discovered that my bedroom experience is extremely limited, you've made it perfectly obvious that you now wish to renegotiate our little deal.'

'Deal?'

'Well, you obviously weren't expecting to give lessons beneath the sheets,' she quipped, concentrating on her coffee cup so that she didn't reveal the depth of hurt in her heart. 'Face it, I was *not* what you expected.'

Totally taken aback to find her on the attack, Zak hesitated. 'That's true in a sense, but still I—' He broke off and glanced up angrily as he heard a noise outside the tent. 'I gave orders not to be disturbed by anyone.'

'But I'm not anyone,' a female voice said huskily and a woman slid through the tent flap, a smile of expectation on her face as she posed provocatively in the doorway.

Zak sucked in a breath. 'Danielle!'

Danielle?

Why was his sister-in-law visiting them in the desert?

Emily glanced between the two of them, sensing tension. And why was she dressed as if she were going to a cocktail party? Her scarlet dress was so short that it exposed an indecent length of thigh and her pouting lips were painted a similar colour.

Remembering his comments to her about her own mode

of dress that day in the *souk*, Emily decided that Crown Prince Zakour al-Farisi could definitely be accused of being a hypocrite. If this was the way his sister-in law dressed, then why had he frowned in disapproval at her ankle-length cotton dress?

On the other hand there was no denying that Danielle was a stunningly beautiful woman in a dark, exotic way, her hair snaking down over one shoulder as glossy and rich as melted chocolate.

'You ordered me home, Zak.' She gave a feline smile. 'Well, here I am. Home.'

Zak's eyes glittered dark with unconcealed anger. 'I ordered you back to Kazban.'

'And when I arrived, I found you were gone,' she said huskily, her smile all feminine temptation.

Snuggled down on the cushions in her white towelling robe, Emily felt distinctly underdressed and insignificant.

Her fragile confidence shattered still further.

'You were not invited home for my benefit, but that of your child,' Zak said, his voice so icily cold that Emily shivered.

If he'd spoken to her in that tone she would have just shrivelled to nothing but Danielle was obviously made of sterner stuff and merely smiled.

'Jamal told me that you were married,' she purred, her eyes sliding to Emily with ill-concealed hostility. 'To be honest I found it hard to believe, in the circumstances.'

Zak rose to his feet in a fluid movement, his expression grim. 'You should *not* be here—'

The woman ignored him, her eyes fixed on Emily, who clutched the neck of her dressing gown self-consciously. 'Don't think that you're anything special. He's married you to punish me.'

Emily suddenly lost her appetite.

Muttering something in Arabic, Zak strode across the Persian carpet, the aggressive set of his jaw leaving no one in any doubt as to his mood. 'Leave before I have you removed.'

Ignoring his chilly tone, Danielle gave a slow smile and laid a hand on his arm. 'I understand why you're angry. I know how frustrating it's been for you,' she purred softly, 'having me so close and not being able to touch. Well, all that's about to change. I made some decisions while I was in Paris.'

Zak looked less than impressed, his handsome face cold and disdainful. 'I am not interested in your decisions,' he bit out, but she lifted an eyebrow and her tongue snaked out and moistened her lower lip.

'No?' Her eyes dropped to his mouth in blatant invitation. 'Not even when they involve you?'

'Your decisions are your own,' Zak replied harshly, turning from her and striding back across the tent, seemingly creating as much distance as possible between himself and the woman who was gazing at him with blatant longing.

'Zak—'

'You should *not* be here.'

Danielle raised an eyebrow towards Emily. 'You mean because of her?' She gave a dismissive shrug, her expression indifferent. 'We all know this marriage isn't real. How can it be? And if you're worried that I'm jealous, then don't be. You're a virile man, Zak, I've never expected you to behave like a monk. Do you think I don't know why you married her?'

Zak sucked in a breath, a warning glittering in his black eyes. 'Danielle—'

'You are still determined to punish me for my mistake.' Suddenly she lifted a hand to her chest and her eyes brimmed with tears. 'I understand how badly I hurt you. But did you really think that this—' she waved a hand at Emily '—that *this* would solve anything?'

Emily sat frozen to the spot.

She'd known that their marriage was a business arrangement.

But it hadn't occurred to her before now that Zak might have another woman in his life.

For some reason that she couldn't identify, the knowledge made her feel sick.

And Zak hadn't so much as glanced in her direction. All his attention was focused on Danielle, and that was hardly surprising, Emily thought dully. The woman was stunning.

'You made your choice, Danielle,' Zak said harshly, 'and now I am free to make mine.'

'And that is what this is all about, of course. As I said, you are punishing me.' Her voice was soft and seductive. 'But now we're even.' Danielle's eyes swivelled to Emily and her gaze was mocking. 'She's very sweet. But not at all your usual type.'

Zak's eyes narrowed and he finally looked at Emily. 'No,' he agreed softly, his eyes resting on her hectically flushed cheeks. Some of the tension seemed to leave him. 'Not at all my usual type.'

His tone was suddenly thoughtful and Danielle shrugged dismissively.

'Your father has always hoped that we would marry. And you were always determined to be your own man.' Her full red mouth curved into a predatory smile. 'I think you've made your point, Zak. We can move on.'

Zak surveyed her in brooding silence and then he nodded sharply. 'I agree. I will return to Kazban today. I should have acted on this before now. I have left it too long.'

Danielle smiled enticingly. 'Then I'll see you back at the palace,' she cooed and Zak snapped his fingers to summon the servants.

As the other woman left the tent Emily felt the confidence ooze out of her.

He obviously couldn't wait to return to the palace, and,

after last night, who could blame him? How could she possibly compete with someone like Danielle?

Feeling that she ought to say something, she forced a smile. 'Obviously you and she have history.'

Zak muttered something in Arabic, pacing across the length of the tent to release the tension that had built inside him. 'It was I who brought her to Kazban ten years ago.'

He made the announcement like a confession and Emily's heart plummeted still further. 'Oh—I see—'

'I doubt it very much.' Zak sucked in a breath, looking like a man at the limits of his patience. 'I need to return to Kazban immediately.'

'Of course.' Emily's tone was flat as she struggled to hide her disappointment.

What had she expected? That he'd keep her here? That they could have a repeat of last night?

This wasn't romance, she reminded herself bleakly. This was business.

The following week seemed to be an endless stream of receptions and formal dinners and at every public event Danielle was there, her heavily made-up eyes fixed on Zak.

Apart from being seated at his side during those dinners, Emily hardly saw Zak. He was either with his father or shut in his office with Sharif so she spent the daylight hours teaching Jamal and playing with him in the beautiful courtyard garden, or going for rides in the desert.

At night she slept alone in a suite of rooms that she could get lost in.

She had no idea where Zak slept, but if Danielle's smug expression was anything to go by she had a fairly good idea.

Why had he married her?

Why hadn't he just married Danielle?

Finally, sitting stiffly by his side at yet another tedious reception, she took matters into her own hands.

Not stopping to question why it should matter to her, she

put a hand on his arm, smiling an apology to the foreign ambassador who was seated to his left. 'I need to talk to you.'

He didn't glance in her direction, instead reaching for his wineglass.

She gritted her teeth. 'I want a divorce.'

Lean brown fingers paused in mid air. 'You have a strange line in dinner-party conversation,' he drawled, his tone lethally soft as he finally turned to look at her.

At least she'd finally caught his attention.

'Since I don't see you at any other time of the day, I'm forced to take whatever opportunity I can.' She smiled across the table at the Minister for Tourism whom she'd already met on several occasions, her relaxed expression concealing the serious nature of the conversation.

'I do not wish to have this conversation in public.' His tone was icy cold and she tightened her grip on her fork, refusing to be intimidated.

'Better in public than not at all. You've been ignoring me and I *hate* that. I want a divorce.'

He lifted his wine, his hand totally steady. 'You can't have a divorce. We have an agreement.'

'Our agreement didn't include you taking a mistress. I won't be humiliated like this.'

He stared at her with naked incredulity. 'Run that past me again?'

She shifted under the heat of that shimmering black gaze, wishing she'd kept her thoughts to herself until she'd been given the opportunity to speak to him in private. 'Well, it's perfectly obvious that you're sleeping with Danielle,' she muttered and Zak lifted an eyebrow, an ironic gleam in his dark eyes.

'One night in my bed and suddenly you are an expert on sexual relationships?'

The reminder of that night caused her to flinch with pain. 'If you find me lacking in expertise then you have only yourself to blame,' she said tightly. 'I haven't had much opportunity to practise.'

There was a throbbing silence and suddenly everything around her faded into the background.

She was aware only of him.

Black eyes clashed with hers and she heard his sharp intake of breath. Then he rose to his feet in a decisive movement, ignoring the fact that silence had descended on the long table.

Without offering a single explanation to his guests, he extended a hand in her direction and Emily flushed, aware that everyone was looking at them and totally unaccustomed to being the focus of attention.

'I just wanted a conversation,' she muttered, 'not a scene.'

'Strange,' Zak murmured silkily, his voice for her ears alone. 'I thought what you wanted was more practice.'

She turned scarlet and he virtually dragged her from the room without glancing left or right, indifferent to the buzz of speculation that greeted their hasty departure.

Emily gave a shiver of anticipation and felt weakness seep through her limbs. Since that one night at the oasis they hadn't been alone together for a single moment.

Until now—

Ignoring the guards and the servants who bowed and scraped and scurried out of their way, Zak strode down endless corridors and up stairs until she reached a section of the palace that she hadn't visited before.

'Where are we?'

'My apartment,' he informed her, flinging open a door and striding inside, still dragging her with him.

Once inside, he slammed the doors closed and turned to face her.

'So what is this nonsense about Danielle?'

Emily swallowed, rendered speechless by the fierce burn in his black eyes.

He was just so attractive, she thought helplessly. And she

was utterly pathetic. Behaving like a jealous female when she had no reason to be jealous.

Only someone in love would be jealous.

And she certainly wasn't in love.

She—she—

She stared at him in horror, rejecting the only plausible justification for her emotional reaction to the fact that Zak was spending time with Danielle.

She didn't care about Zak. She didn't.

'I thought—' Suddenly she was having trouble breathing. 'It's just that I haven't seen you since we arrived back and Danielle is always smiling—'

He lifted a dark eyebrow. 'And you assumed that I was responsible for that smile?'

'You married me to make her jealous.'

A muscle flickered in his jaw. 'I married you because it suited me to do so. And because it would send a message to Danielle that I am not available.'

Emily felt a flicker of hope. 'You spend one night with me—a night during which you choose to try and lose yourself in the desert as an alternative to sleeping with me. Then we come back here and I don't see you. And every time I turn around Danielle is there with that look on her face. What am I supposed to think?'

Zak stared at her, his black eyes shimmering with disbelief. 'That I was giving you space?'

'Oh.' Emily stared at him blankly, totally thrown by his unexpected defence. 'Why would you do that?'

'I thought I was being considerate,' he said dryly, dark eyes raking her face, 'but evidently my sentiments were misplaced.'

Emily felt butterflies take off in her stomach, their wild dance leaving her trembling. When she spoke, her voice was little more than a squeak. 'I don't think I need quite as much space as you've been giving me.'

He tensed, his dark eyes locked on hers. 'How much space?'

She spread her hands in a nervous gesture. 'None?'

He sucked in a breath and raked long fingers through his sleek, dark hair. 'I have had a long day,' he said hoarsely. 'I'm going to take a shower. And then we will talk some more.'

He strode out of the room leaving her staring after him, ready to scream with frustration.

Talk?

Hadn't he listened to a word she'd said?

She didn't want to *talk*.

She paced the length of the enormous living room, hearing the hiss of the shower coming from somewhere in the background.

Why hadn't he just grabbed her?

She'd just decided that she was destined to a life of frustration when she looked up and saw him standing there, naked except for a towel looped low around his hips.

Her mouth dried and her heart did a flip.

Her eyes fixed on his broad chest and then slid down his flat abdomen, following the tantalizing trail of dark curls that disappeared under the towel, before lifting to his face.

Raw passion burned in his eyes and she moved towards him, her heart thumping.

He sucked in a breath. 'You were very distant after our night together. Flippant. And I know I hurt you.'

'Not for long.'

His jaw tightened. 'I had never hurt a woman before—'

'Is that why you stayed away from me?'

'Despite what you may think about me, I was very shocked that you were a virgin. And I was angry,' he admitted in a hoarse tone, lifting a hand and stroking her hair away from one bare shoulder. 'Angry with you for giving away something so precious, so lightly, and angry with myself for not believing you. You deserved better.'

Better?

How much better could it have been?

'It doesn't matter, Zak.' She placed a hand on his chest and felt him tense. Suddenly she realized that he was afraid to touch her. Which meant that she was going to have to take the initiative.

Without bothering to speak again, she leaned forward and pressed her mouth against his muscular shoulder, her tongue flickering out to taste the heat of his skin.

There was a moment of pulsing tension and then he gave a rough exclamation and hauled her against him.

His mouth came down on hers with a searing passion and she gave a whimper of relief, just desperate for him to make love to her the way he had in the desert.

Every night since then she'd lain awake in her bed remembering just how it had felt and the anticipation had risen to fever pitch so that when she finally felt his hands on the zip of her dress she gave a moan of encouragement.

The fabric of her dress was so heavy that it slid to the floor, leaving her in only her very brief, silky underwear.

'Your dress was beautiful but I *definitely* prefer you without clothes,' he informed her huskily, his eyes sliding down her almost naked body with a gratifying amount of male appreciation.

Feeling unusually bold, Emily reached out a hand and jerked his towel and his mouth curved into a sexy smile as she let it fall to the floor.

'*Now* look what you've done,' he said softly, sweeping her into his arms and carrying her across to the enormous bed. He laid her down gently and came down on top of her, potently male and very much the one in control.

She felt her whole body tingle with anticipation and gasped as his mouth fastened over the tip of one creamy breast. Sensation exploded through her body like fireworks and she arched against him. He was hot and hard and so aroused that just feeling him against her made her shift her hips in an agony of frustration.

'You are so impatient, *azîz*,' he groaned, trailing hot kisses down her trembling body, 'and I just love the fact that you want me as much as I want you. I was trying to stay away from you. I even put you in your own apartment because I didn't trust myself to have you in mine and not touch you.'

'I want you to touch me,' Emily assured him breathlessly, twisting and turning as he turned her body into a writhing mass of sensation. 'Zak, please—'

'No.' His voice was a throaty growl and he kissed her briefly before lifting his head to look at her, his breathing unsteady. 'Last time I hurt you. That will *not* happen again.'

And he continued to tease her, introducing her to a level of sensuality that she'd never even dreamed of. With the skilled flick of his tongue and the expert touch of his fingers he drove her to fever pitch, until she was literally begging for the ultimate satisfaction.

She reached down and closed her fingers around his rampant arousal and felt the immediate tension in his hard body as he responded to her touch. His mouth came down on hers with savage urgency and he kissed her with an erotic intimacy that drove her to a state of such intolerable excitement that she felt just *desperate*.

'Zak, *please*.' She sobbed her plea against his beautiful, clever mouth. 'I need you now.'

He shifted so that he was above her, his eyes glittering midnight-black as he stared down at her, his breathing distinctly unsteady. 'I *love* the fact that you are so responsive. And I love the fact that I'm the only man who has ever seen you like this—'

His words jarred slightly, but she was so out of control, so utterly frantic that she couldn't concentrate on anything except the burning heat in her pelvis and the hard throb of his masculinity against her. His first gentle thrust into her body made her gasp and he lifted her hips and thrust again, this time not so gently, driving deep inside her, his whole body controlling and possessing her.

Emily cried out and wrapped her legs around him, instinctively trying to draw him closer. He felt deliciously hard and hot, the power of his masculinity driving her towards that distant point that her body craved.

'You feel *so* good—' His voice thickened with desire, he brought his mouth down on hers again, his tongue sliding into her mouth in an erotic imitation of his more intimate possession of her body.

She slid her arms round his back, feeling the dampness of his skin over the hardness of muscle, feeling the power of his thrust as he moved deeply inside her. And she was aware of nothing except Zak. The incredible closeness, the fierce demands of his body as he joined them together.

And her climax hit with the power of a storm, engulfing her in a pleasure so intense that she cried out his name again and again, her body gripping his so tightly that she heard his harsh groan and felt the hot pulse of his release, deep inside her.

Afterwards Emily lay beneath him, breathless and stunned, waiting for her body to return to something like normal. Every part of her tingled and she could still feel him inside her and she just wanted to stay like that for ever.

For ever.

'Sex with you is so good, *azîz,*' he groaned, gathering her against him and rolling onto his back, his skin damp and his heart rate pounding steadily against her flushed cheek.

Emily clung to him, breathless and dizzy with emotion. Suddenly the truth flashed in front of her like a neon sign.

The reason why she cared whether he had a relationship with Danielle.

She hadn't married Zak for eight million pounds.

She hadn't married Zak for Peter.

She'd married him for her. *Because she loved him.*

CHAPTER TEN

EMILY awoke the next morning to find Zak fully dressed in a dark suit that emphasized his staggering masculinity.

'We need to finish the conversation that we began last night.' His voice was smooth. 'I should have warned you before that Danielle is a master of manipulation. Do not be taken in by her.'

She struggled to sit up, still groggy from the very little sleep he'd allowed her.

'Is she the reason you're so cynical about women?' she ventured. 'Because she played games?'

'Not just Danielle.' His mouth tightened. 'All women play games around me. They always want something and it's almost always related to money or the power that I yield in Kazban. None of the females I meet are ever straightforward.'

Digesting that information and realizing that it probably held a considerable amount of truth, Emily's heart sank. How did one penetrate that degree of suspicion and cynicism? 'Where are you going?'

She didn't quite have the courage to suggest that he came back to bed but she looked at him hopefully.

'I have business to take care of,' he informed her huskily, 'and I am well aware that it is the demands of business that has deprived us of a proper honeymoon. When it is concluded we will go back to the oasis and spend some private time together. And this time we will *not* be disturbed.'

The mere mention of the oasis made her insides melt and her breath suddenly trapped in her throat.

Reading her mind, Zak flashed her a predatory smile. 'Despite the misunderstanding, that night was very special, *ha-*

bibati,' he said softly, 'and we will return as soon as I can arrange it.'

Suddenly Emily realized just how restricted his life was and how little she really knew about him. 'Zak—about our marriage—'

His broad shoulders tensed. 'I want no more talk about our marriage,' he said coldly. 'Last night you were upset. We won't mention it again.'

He was talking about her request for a divorce.

She breathed in slowly. 'H-how can this marriage ever work when you don't love me?' she stammered and he frowned sharply.

'A successful marriage is not about love,' he returned immediately. 'That is why they call it a marriage contract.'

A marriage contract? In a few words he'd reduced her girlish fantasies to a piece of legal jargon.

Emily stared at him in helpless frustration.

He just didn't have a clue when it came to love.

But maybe she could teach him, she thought wistfully. Maybe given time she could rub away some of that cynicism.

While they were at the palace, during the day Emily spent most of her time playing with Jamal. The new nanny was a sweet girl but Jamal always sought her out and she was more than happy to play with him. As for Danielle, there had been no sign of her since the night when Zak had almost carried Emily from the dining table.

Zak left his apartment early every morning and didn't return again until late evening, often after she was already asleep. Judging from the grim expression on his face, Emily deduced that there was obviously some crisis brewing, but whenever she tried to ask if anything was wrong he frowned and changed the subject.

Which was merely a reminder that she wasn't really a part

of his life, she mused, clearing up a pile of toys that Jamal had scattered around their apartment. She might love him, but he certainly didn't love her.

Except in bed.

After that first night in his apartment he joined her every night, his lovemaking so passionate and demanding that often she didn't awake until mid-morning. In fact she was constantly amazed by his stamina. He worked punishing hours, was up half the night positively exhausting her and then sprang out of bed with renewed vigour every morning, leaving her in a shattered heap to sleep off the after effects of his staggering virility.

But she was just relieved to have an outlet for her love. She might not be able to tell him how much she loved him, but every night she *showed* him and their sex life was just amazing.

And their happiness did not go unnoticed.

After one, particularly long evening function when she had been longing to get back to their apartment, a woman came up and kissed her and said something that she didn't understand.

Emily looked at Zak for a translation.

'She is predicting that you will have many healthy babies,' Zak drawled, his eyes hooded as he looked down at her. 'Once again you have gone a very interesting shade of pink.'

Emily wondered whether she ought to point out that it wasn't the thought of having the children that made her blush, but the thought of *making* the child. *With Zak.* 'I love children.'

'That is excellent news,' he returned dryly, 'because as my wife you are naturally expected to produce a healthy number of heirs.'

Emily swallowed. 'We didn't discuss children.'

'As they are generally considered a natural by-product of

marriage, I didn't see the need,' he observed, tightening his long fingers round her wrist and urging her away from the table.

Emily gaped at him, totally staggered by his words. *A by-product of marriage?* She'd never heard children described in such unemotional terms before.

Zak lifted an eyebrow. 'Is something wrong?'

'Yes,' she muttered, smiling sweetly at one of his relatives who was beaming at her from the far corner of the room. 'I can't believe you have such a jaded view of marriage and children.'

'Not jaded. Just practical. And you should be glad about that or we wouldn't be here now.' He looked amused. 'For all your talk of fairy stories, do I need to remind you that you have in fact sold yourself in marriage for the princely sum of eight million pounds? *Not* very romantic, *azîz.*'

Emily swallowed, wondering what he'd say if he knew how she really felt about him.

'Relax.' He bent his dark head closer to hers, his warm breath brushing her cheek. 'You did, after all, land the prince.'

Along with a bucket-load of cynicism.

With his comments about marriage contracts and children being a by-product of marriage, she was fast coming to realize that Zak didn't have a romantic bone in his body.

'You are drifting back into fantasy land, and yet the reality is what matters,' he said firmly. 'Our marriage will work, *azîz*, because it is not clouded by emotion. You claim to like children, which is essential in the woman I marry, and I love the fact that I am the only man you've ever slept with.'

So it was all about ego.

Emily stared at him in helpless frustration, realizing that he truly believed those things to be reasons to marry.

His smile shimmered with sexual promise. 'You will now

smile and bid them goodnight. I wish to take my wife to bed and for that I do *not* require the assistance or felicitations of my relatives.'

A few weeks after they'd returned to the palace, she was curled up in their apartment, reading a book, when Zak came striding in and flourished a tiny box in her direction.

She looked at it warily. 'What's that?'

'Proof that I can be romantic?' His voice was a low, teasing drawl and he leaned forward and dropped a sexy, suggestive kiss on her parted lips. 'Last night was totally amazing, *azîz*. And proof that a marriage that is a business arrangement can work extremely well.'

She swallowed, wondering just what he'd say if she confessed just how much she loved him.

He'd bolt into the desert, she thought dryly, reaching out to take the elaborately wrapped box. Or, knowing Zak, he wouldn't believe her. Because he never seemed to believe *anything* that a woman said to him.

She slipped her finger under the wrapping and revealed a small velvet box.

'Open it,' Zak urged, his eyes blazing with self-satisfaction. 'I chose it myself from our family heirlooms.'

Emily was about to ask what was special about that and then she realized that the Crown Prince probably had an army of staff paid to choose the gifts he presented to women.

Trying not to think about the differences in their lifestyles, she flicked open the box and gave a gasp of pleasure. A heart-shaped pendant nestled in the box, a single diamond so beautiful that it almost dazzled her as it caught the light.

'Oh!'

He lifted it from its box and fastened it around her throat, an extremely smug smile touching his sexy mouth. 'This is a *very* rare diamond, *azîz*,' he assured her. 'Given by my great-grandfather to his wife on the day of their marriage. He loved her *very* much.'

So why was Zak giving it to her? she wondered breathlessly. *Not* love, but still…

'It's beautiful,' she breathed, fingering the stone and gazing at her reflection in the mirror. 'Thank you.'

He lifted her hair to one side and placed a hot, sexy kiss on the back of her neck. 'You are very distracting,' he said huskily. 'I am finding it harder and harder to work knowing that you are waiting here for me.'

It was just sex, she reminded herself firmly, her eyes drifting shut as she felt his arms close around her and she felt the hardness of his body against hers.

She wasn't going to read more into it—

Zak gave a groan and turned her round, stroking her hair away from her flushed cheeks with a gentle hand. 'I want you all to myself,' he murmured, his mouth finding hers in a kiss so full of sensual promise that her knees gave way. 'This afternoon I will take you back to the oasis. I have delayed long enough.'

Emily stared at him. 'The oasis? But your work—'

'Can wait.' He dealt her a sizzling smile. 'I have been parted from my wife for long enough. We leave as soon as possible.'

'But I haven't packed—'

He frowned dismissively. 'That will be taken care of. You just need to bring yourself.'

'But Jamal—' She bit her lip and looked at him pleadingly. 'I wouldn't want to leave him here. Danielle doesn't seem to spend any time with him at all.'

By contrast, Emily had been spending every day with the child and she knew that he needed her.

Zak stared down at her, amusement in his glittering dark gaze. 'I tell you that I wish to be alone with you, and you wish to take the child?'

She coloured deeply. 'Just for the days,' she said hastily and a wry smile touched his firm mouth.

'I had plans for the days, too,' he informed her in a dry

tone, 'but if you wish to take my little nephew, then so be it. He will accompany us. Along with his nanny, who can keep him occupied.' He stroked her face with a gentle finger. 'I intend to keep you *very* busy, *azîz*.'

They arrived at the oasis by late afternoon and an army of servants had prepared everything for their stay.

A meal awaited them and Emily fed Jamal, bathed him and read him a story and eventually made her way back to the tent that was their bedroom.

Just being back in that room made her cheeks warm. The memory of what had happened in that exact room was so vivid that her whole body heated just from looking at the bed.

Zak was sitting at the table, flicking through some papers, a frown on his handsome face as he concentrated.

Even knowing that he didn't love her, she felt amazingly contented.

'How long are we staying?' Emily asked and Zak looked up, his eyes narrowed.

'You don't like the desert?'

'Actually I love it,' she confessed and he sat back, a curious expression in his eyes.

'It pleases me to hear that,' he said quietly, brushing her cheek with the back of his hand. 'This place is special to me also because it is the home of my ancestors and the home of my heart. It is also the place where you first gave yourself to me, *azîz*. And the memory of that stays with me.'

The memory stayed with her too.

She smiled shyly. 'So how long can we stay?'

'Until business dictates that we return,' he said calmly, snapping his fingers at one of the servants, who immediately left the tent and returned carrying plates of food and jugs of wine. 'Come. Let's relax and eat.'

Emily settled herself down on the cushions and glanced at Zak, wondering if she'd ever be able to look at him without getting butterflies in her stomach. He was impossibly good-looking and almost unbearably sexy and just knowing what he could do to her in bed made her feel weak with longing.

She dragged her eyes away from him and tried to concentrate on the food.

'If it is any consolation, you have a similar effect on me, *azîz*,' he drawled lightly, dismissing the servants with a jerk of his head and reaching for the jug of wine. 'I, too, spend my days dreaming about our nights.'

'Oh—' Mortified that he'd read her thoughts so easily, Emily took a large sip of wine and felt the warmth flow through her veins. 'Tomorrow Jamal wants to go riding. Will you come?'

He gave a lazy smile. 'You are a coward, Emily. Every night in my bed you are a wanton, begging for my touch, but in the light of day you blush and look at the floor, at the ceiling—anywhere except at me.'

Because she was so afraid of giving herself away. In the darkness she often mouthed those secret words that she was afraid to voice in daylight.

'I haven't really seen you during the day,' she pointed out, trying to keep her tone light. 'You've been working.'

'But now I am not working,' he assured her smoothly, 'and I wish to get to know my wife.'

'Most people get to know each other before they get married.'

He gave a cynical smile. 'Actually I disagree. I think many people think that they know each other before they get married, but then in time each discovers many things about the other and becomes disillusioned. Before a marriage takes place people can pretend to be many things but the act usually drops at some point. We knew the truth about each other before we married.'

She swallowed and put her wine down on the table. 'You

still believe that I knew about Peter—that I lied to you when I said that I truly didn't know.'

'It doesn't matter.' He shrugged dismissively, a frown touching his forehead. 'We each had a reason for marrying, Emily. I am satisfied. You are satisfied. We will speak of it no more.'

But she *wanted* to speak of it. She *wanted* him to believe her. But his view of the world was just too cynical. She looked at him helplessly, wanting to defend herself but knowing that his suspicion of her sex was too deep-rooted to be easily shifted. 'Was it just Danielle?'

He frowned. 'Was what just Danielle?'

'Who made you believe that women play games and manipulate? Was it just her that made you so cynical?'

He gave a short laugh. 'Emily, women have played games with me since I was old enough to walk. I have wealth and influence and there is always someone who wants a piece of that.'

She toyed with the food on her plate. 'You really think it's impossible that someone would love you for yourself?'

He shrugged. 'In my position I never anticipated marrying for love. I'm not even sure that love exists.'

Emily swallowed back her disappointment. 'Y-you've never loved anyone?'

He shook his head. 'And evidently you haven't either,' he drawled softly, 'or you would not have been a virgin when I took you to my bed.'

'I was waiting for the right man,' she confessed and his eyes narrowed.

'And then you met me—'

And he *was* the right man, but obviously there was no way she could ever tell him that.

Emily lowered her eyes, afraid that he might read the truth.

After that first day all the other days followed a similar

pattern. They rose late, rode or drove into the desert, played with Jamal and then dined and talked late into the night.

And then they retired to bed.

For Emily it was a blissful existence. So what if he didn't love her? Zak was proving himself to be amazingly attentive and thoughtful.

Each day he brought her little gifts to amuse her and he was extremely good company. Incredibly clever but also amusing and charming and she just loved being with him.

And as they spent time together he opened up more and more and she started to understand the almost intolerable pressure that had been placed on him since childhood.

If his attentions were required elsewhere then she rode with Jamal.

'Uncle Zak says I can ride into the desert as long as we don't go far. He's going to join us when his business is finished,' Jamal told her one day as they set off, digging his heels into his pony and encouraging it to canter.

Emily urged her horse forward and caught up with the little boy. 'You're an amazing rider.'

'Uncle Zak taught me,' Jamal told her proudly. 'My mother didn't want me to ride, she says it's dangerous, but Uncle Zak said that I must learn.'

'Well, you certainly paid attention,' Emily said, watching as the child sat effortlessly on his pony, totally relaxed.

'You see over there?' He gestured far into the distance. 'There are caves. There are stories about them. Some people say that they're so deep that no one has ever found the end of them.'

Emily gave a shudder. 'I thought you hated the dark?'

'Only in the palace,' he told her. 'In the desert it's different and I'd love to go to the caves. One day I'm going to ride all the way there by myself.'

'Well, not when I'm in charge of you, you're not,' Emily said quickly, shooting a reproving look in his direction. Exploring a dark cave with no end wasn't her idea of fun.

'It isn't that far,' Jamal said, his eyes still fixed longingly on the horizon. 'And I'm older now. I could look after you—'

'No, thanks.' Emily kicked her horse into a canter. 'You can do that trip with Zak.'

And right on cue she heard the thunder of hooves and Zak galloped towards them on a very over-excited Sahara.

Jamal's face lit up. 'Can I ride him, Uncle Zak. Please?'

'No one has ever ridden Sahara but me,' Zak said gently, 'but perhaps when you are older.'

Jamal's face fell and then lit up again. 'Can we go to the caves?'

'Not today.' Zak shook his head and glanced at the darkening sky with a frown. 'It is already growing late and the distance is too far. That trip must wait for another time.'

'But I want to go to the caves.'

'And so you will,' Zak promised. 'Another time.'

Jamal's face crumpled and he kicked his pony into a canter and rode off in the opposite direction while Zak gave a sigh of exasperation.

'It seems that I am destined to say "no" to his every request,' he commented and Emily smiled.

'He's a typical five year old. Trying it on.'

Zak looked at her, totally relaxed as the powerful horse pranced under him. 'You are extremely good with the child.'

'I love him,' Emily said simply, her eyes following the little boy, checking that he was all right. 'He's great. Warm, friendly and full of energy and enthusiasm. And I love it here.' Her eyes tracked the horizon, taking in the play of light on the sand dunes, and she smiled. 'I always loved the beach as a child. This is like a giant beach with no sea.'

Zak didn't smile. Instead he watched her, a thoughtful frown touching his face, and then he spun Sahara around and cantered steadily after the child.

Emily followed at a slower pace, wondering what she'd said to bring that frown to his face.

But she had no chance to question him because they caught up with Jamal and rode together, the earlier tension forgotten in the thrill of a fast gallop.

That night at dinner she found herself telling Zak things that she'd never told another human being. About how alone she'd felt growing up without her parents. About moving out so that she could give Peter and Paloma some space.

He listened intently, his brilliant dark eyes fastened on hers as she hesitantly revealed parts of herself that she'd never revealed before.

Eventually he took her to bed, but his lovemaking seemed more gentle, less frantic than usual, and Emily felt something different in his skilled touch.

When he curved her against him, she could feel his heart pounding under her hand.

'You will *never* feel alone again, *habibati*.'

He delivered that statement like a command and Emily tilted her head so that she could look at him, touched that he acknowledged her feelings and amused that he made it sound like an order.

'I don't feel lonely,' she said softly, aware of every inch of him pressed against her.

Whether she liked it or not, he was part of her. And she closed her eyes, trying to prepare herself mentally for pain. Because pain was inevitable. What other outcome could there be when he so clearly didn't love her?

Zak stared down at her sleeping form and felt his insides tighten.

Never had he been so affected by a woman as he was by Emily.

It was just sex, he told himself, reaching for a pair of trousers and pulling them on. *Incredibly good sex*, but sex after all.

He moved towards the entrance of the tent intending to

get some fresh air, but something made him look back and his gaze was once again held by her sleeping figure.

As usual her unruly blonde hair was trespassing across both pillows and her smooth cheeks were pink from the sun.

He frowned at that, making a mental note to order her to wear a hat more often. He knew only too well just what an extreme effect that desert heat could have on the unwary.

She looked like a sleeping princess and his jaw tightened as he considered all that he'd learned about her in the past few weeks.

She had evidently had an *extremely* lonely childhood and the knowledge made his insides twist. Given that she had known very little affection in her life, it was hardly surprising that she dreamed of princes and palaces.

And what a disappointment he must be to her, he reflected wryly.

She'd wanted romance and been presented with a business proposition.

Business—

Zak stilled, his eyes sliding down the curve of her hip.

Not business—

With a sharp intake of breath, he was forced to acknowledge the truth. That no matter what Emily had done, he was in love with her.

Which presented him with something of a problem, because she was most definitely not in love with him. She'd married him to clear her brother's debts. And the fact that she adored sex with him didn't change the fact that she'd married him under pressure.

Zak swallowed a groan of frustration.

For the first time in his life he found himself in love and the woman in question had wanted nothing more than to escape from him. The irony of the situation was not lost on him.

On the other hand she *was* married to him, he reminded

himself, which meant that he had every day and every night to persuade her to love him as he loved her.

And starting tomorrow that was *exactly* what he was going to do.

They were eating breakfast the following morning when there was a commotion outside the tent.

Zak looked up with a frown and Emily felt her heart sink.

Surely it wasn't Danielle. She'd been anticipating trouble from the woman since the day they'd arrived back at the palace, but as time had passed she'd started to relax.

So she was astonished when the flap of the tent was pulled aside and her brother entered.

'Peter?' Taken by surprise, Emily just stared and stared and then she gave a cry of delight, scrambled to her feet and ran towards her brother, arms outstretched. 'Oh, Peter, *Peter*. I've been so worried about you.'

'Em—' His voice cracked slightly and she burst into tears and clutched him tightly and then withdrew, her expression concerned as she studied him closely.

'You've lost weight,' she said, her breathing jerky as she struggled to contain her tears. 'Where have you been?'

'Em—' Peter looked down at her with a shake of his head. 'I can't believe you've been here all this time.'

'I rang you and rang you—'

He gave a groan and closed his eyes briefly. 'And I wasn't there—I'm sorry.'

'Where *were* you—and why didn't you tell me you were going away? Have you been ill?'

He hesitated and pulled away from her, his features tense. 'Not exactly.' Peter kept his arm round her and shifted his gaze to Zak, his expression suddenly fierce. *'You kept her here.'*

Zak stood still, muscular legs set apart in his usual aggressive stance, surveying the proceedings with unshakeable cool.

'Naturally.'

Peter's arm dropped from her shoulders and he took a step forward, his fists raised, and suddenly the tent was full of armed guards who seized Peter and held him captive.

'No!' Emily looked at them in horror. 'Let him go! Zak?'

She appealed to her husband, hands outstretched, and he lifted a hand and dismissed the guards in one brief gesture.

'Zak?' Peter looked at her in disbelief and then looked at the prince and gave a contemptuous laugh. 'So it's true, then. When I arrived in Kazban they told me that you'd— that you were married.'

Zak's handsome face was expressionless. 'Emily is my wife, that's true.'

Peter gave an agonized groan and covered his face with his hands. 'I can't believe it—I can't believe you did that—' His hands slid from his face and he shook his head, his face a mixture of remorse and condemnation. 'I was the one you wanted. I was the one who owed you money. She isn't your type of woman, couldn't you see that?' Peter ran a hand over his face and let out a long breath. 'Couldn't you see that she was innocent? It was *me* you wanted,' he grated roughly, 'but you took her instead, didn't you? You punished her for my wrongs.'

Emily caught hold of his arm. 'Peter, listen—'

'And you were the one who sent your sister in your place,' Zak returned, his tone cold and hard as he fixed glittering black eyes on her brother. 'You gave her to me.'

'I sent her to deliver a message!' Peter was breathing rapidly now and Emily looked at him in concern.

'Peter, it really doesn't—'

'She delivered your message,' Zak said calmly, his gaze not shifting from Peter's tortured face.

'And then you wouldn't let her leave.'

'She was my collateral.'

'Collateral.' Peter gave another groan. 'Emily is a totally innocent young girl—'

'Not so innocent,' Zak drawled harshly. 'You'll no doubt

be pleased to hear that she defended you all the way. She'd showed as little conscience about the debt as you did.'

'She defended me because I'm the only family she has in the world and because that's the sort of person she is,' Peter hissed through gritted teeth, 'not because she approved of the debt. Emily didn't even know about the debt. She thought I'd made some bad investments and the return was poor. She didn't know I'd lost the money. It wasn't exactly something I was proud of and I wasn't about to admit it to my little sister.'

There was an achingly long silence and Zak was unusually still, not a muscle moving in his powerful physique as he digested that information.

'Then what induced you to send her in your place?' he asked harshly, his broad shoulders suddenly rigid with tension. 'You *knew* I would never let her go.'

Peter let out a jerky breath. 'I assumed that you'd see how innocent she was. No one who knows Emily could ever think she was guilty of anything dishonest. She dreams of fairy tales and happy endings. She teaches little children and she can't wait to have about ten of her own. She's never done *anything* corrupt in her life. I assumed you'd be able to see that.'

Zak's gaze swivelled to Emily and a strange expression flickered across his handsome face. 'Unfortunately for you I have so rarely encountered innocence in my life,' he said softly, 'that when I finally did, I failed to spot it. Until it was too late.'

His eyes were fixed on Emily and she felt her heart thud uncomfortably.

Peter gave a groan. 'The debt was mine.'

Worried to death about the anxiety in his face, Emily hurried forward and took his hands, eager to reassure him on that score. 'Zak has cancelled the debt, Peter,' she said quietly, noting with alarm how cold his hands were. 'You no longer owe him the money.'

Peter looked at her in blank incomprehension and then he shook his head. 'No!' He transferred his gaze to Zak and then back to his sister. 'That's why you did it, isn't it? You married him so that he'd cancel the debt—'

'Peter—'

'And there's no need to ask what was in it for you.' Peter held Emily's hands tightly and gave a contemptuous laugh as he looked at the prince. 'Let me tell you something about my sister. I'm all the family she has and I have to confess that it isn't much. She's spent her whole life dreaming about love and babies and happy families—'

'Peter, please—' Emily attempted to stop him but Peter wasn't looking at her. He was looking at Zak.

'I'm her brother and we don't exactly talk about things like that, but even I know that she's never been to bed with anyone because she was waiting for the right man. She was dreaming of *love*, Your Highness. And what did you give her?'

'Peter, that's enough.' Emily jerked his arm and forced him to look at her. 'It was my choice to marry the prince. Mine. Nobody made me.'

Peter shook his head. 'I know everything that happened, Em,' he groaned, guilt written clearly over his face. 'I was in Kazban long enough to hear about your attempts to escape. I know about the number of times you called and called, desperate to speak to me, and I'm sorry I wasn't there for you. But I'm here now—' he glared at the prince '—and I'm taking you home with me. Away from this sham of a marriage.'

Emily swallowed hard. 'Peter—' She said his name tentatively. 'Peter, this is my home now.'

Peter shook his head. 'You're just saying that because of the money, but there's no need to worry. I've made some mistakes but I haven't totally lost my touch,' he said bitterly. 'I have his money in full, plus interest payments, so now he can release you.'

Emily frowned. 'You have the money?'

Peter gave a funny little smile. 'Aren't you even going to ask me why I took eight million pounds?' He looked at Zak, his gaze challenging. 'You see? Her love for me is so unquestioning she doesn't even bother asking why I did it.'

'I am convinced of your sister's unimpeachable character,' Zak said flatly. 'There is no longer any need for you to prove it to me.'

Peter's chin lifted. 'So you'll grant her a divorce, then.'

Zak looked at Emily, a muscle flickering in his lean cheek. 'If that is what she desires.'

Emily felt her stomach lurch. She didn't want a divorce. But how could she tell Peter of that without revealing the extent of her feelings to Zak? And she just knew that he wouldn't want to know that she loved him. Zak thought that they had a business arrangement and if that was what it took to stay married to him then she was more than happy to go along with that.

She consoled herself with the fact that Zak couldn't divorce her. He needed her to keep Danielle at bay. He needed a wife.

Resolving to confess all to Peter as soon as they were alone, she changed the subject away from divorce. 'So why did you need the money, Peter? And where's Paloma?'

Peter tensed. 'Paloma is in hospital,' he said finally, a weary expression crossing his face as he glanced at her. 'She's been there since the day after you flew to Kazban.'

'In hospital?' Emily looked at him with shock and concern. 'But what's the matter with her?'

Peter hesitated. 'She has a type of depression,' he muttered. 'And because of it, she's been spending money. Lots of it. And shoplifting.'

Emily gaped at him. Paloma had spent the money?

'She ran up huge debts without me knowing,' Peter said quietly. 'Huge sums of money. That day I took you to the airport, she'd been arrested for shoplifting. I had to go to the police station and bail her out. There was no way I could have gone to Kazban. I had to be there for Paloma.'

'Well, of course you did,' Emily said immediately, her face creased with worry. 'What happened?'

Peter sighed. 'Being arrested just finished her off. She had some sort of mental breakdown and they admitted her to hospital. She's been there ever since, and I've been with her. Day and night. And when she slept I played the money markets.' He turned and looked at Zak. 'Very successfully. The money is back in your account. I apologize for using it in that way but I was desperate.'

Emily was still looking at him. 'And Paloma? Is she better?'

Peter shrugged. 'They think so, but it's going to be a long haul. I need to get back to her.' His eyes were still on Zak. 'And I intend to take my sister home with me—'

'Peter, wait—' But before Emily could say anything more the tent flap was pulled aside and a group of men entered, each bowing low before the prince.

Emily didn't understand anything they said but she could tell it was serious from the amount of hand waving and the grim expression on Zak's face.

Finally he spoke, his voice calm in comparison to the panic going on around him.

'It seems that this is a day for family problems.' His gaze flickered to Emily. 'Danielle has left the palace and returned to France with a man she met there.'

Emily gasped. 'But Jamal—?'

Zak's mouth tightened. 'She has chosen a new life over her child. And I must of course return home. There is yet more scandal brewing and I want to minimize the stress on my father.'

Danielle had left?

But that meant that—

Emily felt panic churn inside her. He'd married her to

keep Danielle from causing trouble. If the woman was gone from his life, then his reason for marrying her was gone.

'Zak—' She reached out a hand, desperate to speak to him on his own, but he had already turned away and was striding towards the door.

'I will arrange for transport to return you to Kazban and then England,' he delivered over his shoulder, and then he disappeared through the flap and was gone.

Gone.

Emily stared after him in dismay and then turned to follow him. 'Zak!'

'Emily, wait!' Peter grabbed her arm, his face covered in relief. 'The guy has just told you that you can go back to England.'

'But I don't want to go back to England,' she mumbled, shaking him off, feeling the misery well up inside her. 'I *love* Zak. And I want to stay married to him.'

'You love him?' Peter was struck dumb. 'But the guy forced you to marry him—'

'I married him because I loved him,' Emily said simply. 'And I know he doesn't love me but I didn't care. And I still don't care.'

Peter stared at her. 'I don't know what to say.'

Emily gave a wan smile. 'Nothing to say. He had his own reasons for marrying me and those reasons have gone now, so he is happy to give me a divorce.'

Even saying the words was intolerably painful.

'I'm sorry—'

'It isn't your fault. Whether you'd come here or not, Danielle would still have left and he wouldn't have needed me any more.'

Their marriage had been a business arrangement.

Peter shook his head. 'I don't understand any of this. Does this mean that you're coming home with me, or not?'

'Eventually.' Emily tried to pull herself together. 'I can't leave with you now because Jamal will need me if Zak's gone—' She swallowed. 'You go home, Peter. I'll come home when I've sorted things out here.'

CHAPTER ELEVEN

'EMILY, can we go for a ride in the desert this morning?' Jamal jumped up and down on her bed and Emily forced her eyes open.

There'd been no word from Zak and she'd barely slept for the past three days and nights. Obviously he wasn't coming back, she reflected miserably. He'd just assumed that she'd go with Peter. He'd wanted her to go with Peter.

Their marriage contract was ended.

Shaking off the deep depression that threatened, she smiled at the little boy. 'Of course we can go riding in the desert. I'll just get dressed.'

At least riding took her mind off her problems, even if it was only fleeting.

She knew it was only a matter of time before someone arrived to take Jamal back to Kazban, and then her reason for being here would be over.

Until then, she would make the most of being in the desert. The place that was so closely linked with her love for Zak.

She dressed quickly and took the little boy to the stables.

'Can we go to the caves?'

Emily shook her head. 'That is a trip for you to do with Zak,' she told him. 'I don't know the way and it could be dangerous.'

'But it's early in the morning and Zak said that as long as we set off early we could go.'

'But that was when he was with us,' Emily pointed out. 'I wouldn't have a clue how to get there—'

'But you can see them in the distance,' Jamal pleaded and she bent and gave him a hug.

'Zak will take you. He promised. You and I will do a more local trip.'

The little boy's face fell and she was about to say something to cheer him up when one of the staff came hurrying up carrying a satellite phone.

'There is a call for you, my lady—'

Zak—

Her heart thumping with excitement and trepidation, she took the phone and walked back to the tents, anxious for privacy so that they could have a proper conversation. After all, they hadn't spoken at all since Peter's unexpected arrival days earlier.

'Zak?'

'It's Peter.'

'Oh.' Disappointment thudded through her with the force of an express train. *She'd wanted it to be him so badly.* 'Did you arrive home safely?'

'Yes, and I just wanted to check that you're OK. When are you coming home?'

'Soon,' she said evasively, not wanting to face the fact that her marriage was over. Zak obviously wasn't coming back for her. She had no doubt that soon he'd send for Jamal and her reason for staying would be gone.

Trying not to think about that, she talked to Peter about Paloma, ascertained that she was much better and then talked about their plans for the future.

By the time she eventually broke the connection almost half an hour had passed and she realized that Jamal would still be waiting for her to go riding.

Feeling guilty, she hurried back outside, expecting to see him bouncing on the spot impatiently.

There was no sign of him.

'Jamal?' She called his name, a frown on her face as she walked along the paths that criss-crossed the fields and led to the stables. 'Jamal?'

She arrived at the yard and saw the staff clustered together at one end, chattering excitedly.

She suppressed a groan, wondering what mischief Jamal had been up to this time.

'Where is the child?' She addressed the nearest servant and he waved his hand frantically towards the desert.

'Gone. He has gone.'

Emily froze. 'What do you mean he has gone? Gone where?'

'He has gone into the desert, my lady. To the caves.'

Her heart lurched. 'And you let him?'

'He ordered us to let him go, my lady. He is a royal prince. We cannot stop him.'

'He is a royal prince who is five years old,' she spat, whirling round and looking at the others. 'Why didn't any of you go with him?'

They glanced at each other nervously and then one of them waved a hand at the sky. 'Very bad storm coming, my lady—'

Emily looked up impatiently and felt a lurch of fear as she saw the ominous colour of the sky and felt the threatening breath of the wind touch her face. The palm trees swayed and a faint mist of sand was visible above the curve of the dunes.

She'd never been in a desert in a storm, but Jamal had told her about them.

'I have to go after him. Saddle me a horse *now*.'

There was a tense silence and they shook their heads. 'It is too dangerous. The storm is less than an hour away and you will never reach him in time. We must just hope he has reached the caves and has found shelter. After the storm we will go to him.'

'Well, after the storm will be too late,' she said angrily, taking several deep breaths while she tried to work out what to do. A loud stamping and snorting came from one of the stables and she glanced up and her eyes narrowed.

Sahara.

Without communicating her intention to anyone, she sprinted across the yard, grabbed a saddle and a bridle and hurried to his box.

'OK, now I know you don't generally let anyone ride you except Zak,' she said softly, sliding the bolt carefully and walking into his box, 'but this is an emergency.'

The horse sniffed her suspiciously and gave a snort of disgust when he saw the bridle.

'Yes, I know,' Emily crooned, stroking a hand over his silken neck, feeling the powerful muscles under her fingers. 'I know you don't want me to ride you but you're my only hope. I need to be on the fastest horse in the world, and everyone tells me that's you.'

Still talking, she saddled and bridled the horse and led him into the yard.

The staff were staring at her in horrified silence, unable to move. Finally one of them stepped forward.

'You cannot ride that horse, my lady—'

'I have to.' She held tight to Sahara, who was dancing on the spot. 'He's my only chance of reaching Jamal before the storm. Someone give me a leg up.'

The horse was enormous and she had absolutely no chance of vaulting onto him without help.

But no one helped her. They just stared.

'No one has ever ridden that horse except the Crown Prince,' someone said and she gritted her teeth.

'Then it's time we gave him some variety. Now, will one of you help me?'

'I will help you.' From nowhere, Sharif hurried forward, his face lined with worry. 'I have only just heard. They have behaved very badly—they should have gone after the child, no matter how bad their own fears. The prince will be severely angered.'

'Never mind that now. Can you get me on this animal,

Sharif?' Emily muttered, glancing up and thinking that the horse seemed like Everest. Unattainable.

Without further question Sharif put his hands under her knee and lifted her onto the horse in a powerful movement.

The horse snorted and danced and Emily held the reins lightly, her touch gentle.

'It's OK,' she crooned softly, stroking his neck with her hand. 'We're going to find Jamal together.'

'I will inform the prince,' Sharif said quickly, his eyes troubled as he looked at her. 'I wish you good fortune—'

Without waiting to hear the rest of his words, Emily urged Sahara forward and headed for the caves.

'She has gone into the desert? *In a sandstorm?*' His handsome face a mask of incredulity and anxiety, Zak sprang out of the helicopter and strode towards the stables with Sharif hurrying to keep up.

'She went after the child, Your Highness. About an hour before your arrival.'

Zak stopped dead and let out his breath in a hiss. 'Why did no one try and stop the child?'

'Her Highness was taking a telephone call at the time,' Sharif explained, 'and none of the other staff felt able to prevent the child from carrying out his plan. Jamal can be— a difficult child to handle, as you know, Your Highness.'

'Only Emily has the measure of him, it would seem,' Zak returned grimly. 'Why did none of the staff follow him, or at least go with Emily?'

'They were afraid.' Sharif swallowed. 'She took Sahara, Your Highness.'

Zak stopped dead, fear punching his heart like a fist. 'She rode the *stallion*?' His voice was rough with concern and Sharif bowed his head.

'Indeed. Her Highness believed the horse was her only hope of reaching the child in time.'

Zak closed his eyes. He'd had several days to get used to

the idea that Emily was the opposite of everything he'd ever encountered in a woman before. Instead of selfish she was selfless, instead of cold she was warmth and instead of taking she gave.

And this time she was risking her life for a second time to save his wayward little nephew.

The thought that he might have found her only to lose her made him growl in anger. 'I will take the helicopter up again.'

Sharif's eyes widened in dismay. 'Your Highness, you can't—'

'She has taken the fastest horse,' Zak bit out grimly, striding back towards the helipad behind the stables. 'The four-by-four will never reach her in time.'

'But the wind is rising. The risk is enormous—'

'I know the risk, Sharif,' Zak replied harshly, reaching the helicopter and dismissing his guards with a snap of his fingers. 'Which is why I will fly myself.'

'Your Highness—'

Zak turned to his adviser, a man who was almost a father to him. His eyes were fierce and his voice was rough with anxiety. 'We are talking of my nephew and the woman I love, Sharif—'

'So be it.' A light appeared in the other man's eyes. 'In that case, hurry. The storm is approaching fast.'

Emily screwed up her eyes against the wind, holding onto a hunk of Sahara's mane as he galloped full pelt through the desert towards the caves.

Ahead she could see the sky darkening and she knew that time was running out. And still there was no sign of Jamal.

'Where is he, Sahara?' she muttered, squinting at the horizon, looking for something, anything, that might give her a clue as to the little boy's whereabouts.

But she saw nothing except sand. Mountains and valleys of sand threatened by a sky so black that it made her shiver.

It was still daytime and yet it might have been night.

She could see the caves clearly now. Had Jamal reached them?

And then Sahara came to an abrupt halt, rearing up on his hind legs, squealing with fear and surprise.

Taken by surprise, Emily tumbled off his back and landed in the sand.

'Emily?' A wobbly voice came from next to her and she sat up, to find Jamal huddled in a heap next to her.

'Oh, sweetheart—' Weak with relief, she hugged the little boy tightly and then scrambled to her feet, knowing that there was no time to lose.

'We have to get out of here.'

'Em, the pony's gone. He stumbled and I fell off.'

'Never mind that now.' Emily lifted him up and looked around her frantically. 'We need to get to the caves. There's a storm coming, Jamal—'

Already the sand was blowing around them and she tied her scarf round the child's head to protect his eyes, squinting into the distance.

It was too far.

They were never going to make it.

'Sahara!' She shouted for the horse but he snorted wildly and cantered into the distance, excited and frightened by the building storm.

Jamal gave a little sob and snuggled against her, turning his head against the rising wind. 'I'm sorry, Em—'

His choked apology brought a lump to her throat and she hugged him hard. 'Don't worry, darling, we'll be fine,' she promised, but her heart was thudding in her chest and her palms were clammy with fear. There was no way they'd reach the caves without the horse and Sahara was badly frightened and determined not to be caught.

And then she heard it.

A clack-clacking sound. She shielded her eyes and looked

up, her heart surging with relief as she saw the black helicopter settling onto the sand like a giant insect.

'It's Uncle Zak—' Jamal pulled away from her and ran towards the helicopter just as an athletic figure sprang onto the sand.

He was by her side in seconds, his fingers biting into her upper arms as he held her steady. He seemed unbearably tense and she realized that it was the first time she'd ever seen him close to losing his cool.

'Where is Sahara?' His voice was harsh and he gave her a little shake.

'He galloped off,' she said, raising her voice to be heard above the wind. 'The wind frightened him.'

Zak muttered something under his breath and then lifted his fingers to his mouth and whistled sharply. The same whistle he'd used that evening in the *souk.*

Almost immediately the powerful horse galloped up to them and Emily looked at him in amazement.

'Get on.' Zak lifted her bodily into the saddle and then placed Jamal in front of her before vaulting on himself and shouting something at the stallion.

He clamped protective arms around Emily and Jamal and the horse took off at speed, plunging through the sand and the storm towards the safety of the caves.

How the horse could move so fast carrying three of them, Emily didn't know, but somehow they made it to the entrance of the caves and Zak immediately vaulted off and smacked the horse on the rump, sending him deeper into the cave.

'Uncle Zak!' Jamal cried out in fear, glancing back over his shoulder as Sahara pranced deeper into the cave.

'Go!' Zak growled. 'I will join you in a minute.'

Emily had no idea what he was doing but she was so relieved to be out of the storm that she followed his orders without question.

Besides, he so clearly knew what he was doing, whereas she didn't have a clue.

Sahara plodded deeper into the cave and it started to grow darker. Emily swallowed and pulled the horse to a standstill, listening, hoping to hear Zak behind them.

At first there was nothing.

Only the howl of the wind and the eery sound of dripping water in the cave. And then she heard hooves.

'He's found my pony!' Jamal gave a squeal of delight and slid from Sahara's back.

Zak gave him the pony to hold and then stretched up and lifted Emily out of the saddle, lowering her carefully to the ground.

Her body brushed against the hard muscle of his and she gave a shiver of relief, leaning into his strength.

'I can't believe you flew in that.'

He gave a groan and shook his head. 'And I can't believe you rode Sahara in that.'

Her pulse rate increased. 'You're angry that I took your precious horse, but—'

'No.' He gave her a little shake. 'Not because of the risk to Sahara, but because of the risk to you, *azîz.*'

He was worried about her?

'I had to try and get to Jamal,' she said simply, 'and I could see no other way.'

He closed his eyes briefly. 'And for that I am eternally grateful,' he grated, 'because had anything happened to the child—'

'It didn't.' Emily reached up and touched his cheek, feeling the roughness of his jaw under her shaking fingers. 'Thanks to you. If you hadn't come when you did—'

His fingers tightened on her arm. 'We will not think about that.' He stared down at her, and then he looked at Jamal, who was cuddling the pony. 'We must get deeper into the cave.'

Emily looked at him, less than enthusiastic. 'It's very dark—'

Suddenly his eyes lit with amusement. 'This is the girl who abseiled down the side of my palace and rode my half wild stallion through a sandstorm. Are you telling me you're afraid of the dark?'

'Actually, yes.' Her voice was small and he frowned, pulling her against him.

'I will let nothing hurt you,' he said hoarsely. 'Believe that, Emily. You are mine and I will protect you with all that I have, including my life.'

Her heart pattered frantically, but she reminded herself that he was just grateful because she'd tried to save Jamal.

They moved deeper into the cave until finally Zak said that they could rest. 'There is water here and the sand will not penetrate this far,' he said, reaching into his backpack and removing blankets and drinks. He tucked Jamal into a blanket and, showing all the resilience of youth, the child was soon asleep.

Zak flicked on a torch. 'We will wait for the storm to die down and then they will rescue us.'

'Will they? No one would help me rescue Jamal,' Emily said in a hushed voice and his mouth tightened.

'And for that they will be severely punished. If anything had happened to either of you—'

'How did you know where I was?'

Zak settled himself comfortably and pulled her close. 'Sharif called me urgently. I was with my father and the moment I heard I flew myself back to the oasis only to find that you'd taken Sahara and ridden into a sandstorm.' He exhaled sharply and turned to look at her, his eyes glittering dark in the torchlight. 'For the second time in my life I knew real fear.'

'When was the first time?'

He gave a rueful smile. 'When I thought you were about to be crushed to death under Sahara's hooves.'

She touched his arm. 'It's natural to be worried about your nephew—'

'Not just my nephew,' he said softly, lifting a hand and touching her face gently. 'I had expected you to leave with Peter.'

Emily's heart did acrobatics inside her chest. His voice was warm and intimate. *Just for her.* And it made her nerve endings tingle.

'You dashed off so suddenly and I didn't want to leave Jamal without either of us there, especially if there was some scandal involving his mother brewing—' She bit her lip. 'In fact it's my fault he got into trouble, Zak. I was on the phone—'

'And he is a mischief,' Zak interrupted in a dry tone. 'With plenty of staff to look after him, all of whom failed in their duty to him. Unlike you—'

'I love him.'

'I know you do. And I owe you an apology for the way I have treated you, *azîz,*' he groaned, leaning forward and taking her hand in his. 'I have spent so much of my life surrounded by people who are never what they seem that when I finally met someone who was exactly as they seemed, I missed it.'

'It really doesn't matter.'

'You are very forgiving but I would expect no less from you. You told me repeatedly that you were innocent and I refused to believe you and that shames me,' he confessed, his voice rough and intensely masculine. 'I have treated you appallingly and yet still you stay and care for my nephew, even though your own brother has repaid the debt.'

'Having met your sister-in law, I can hardly blame you for being cynical,' she said, touched by his apology.

His black eyes hardened. 'My love for her died when she married my brother. I realized almost immediately that I had been spared from making a serious mistake. Unfortunately the same could not be said of my brother. She tore Raschid apart with her tricks, her deviousness and her constant demands for money. She was directly responsible for his premature death.'

Realising that he was confiding in her for the first time, Emily snuggled closer. 'What happened?'

'Raschid found himself torn between the demands of his people and the demands of his wife. During one of her tantrums he followed her into the desert in a fierce storm. His vehicle turned over and he was killed.'

Emily gave a murmur of sympathy, hardly able to imagine how Zak must have felt.

'Once my brother was buried she turned her attention back to me. She cried and wept and told me that she'd made a mistake marrying Raschid. Apparently I was her one and only love.' His mouth twisted in a cynical smile as he finally turned to look at her.

'But that isn't love! She clearly didn't love either of you,' Emily blurted out, horrified by the story. 'Only herself. That's awful! Coming between brothers like that. Frankly I'm amazed that you allowed her houseroom.'

His broad shoulders tensed. 'She remained in the family only because of her link with Jamal.' A muscle worked in his lean jaw. 'And my father always entertained a hope that I would marry her because he felt that I might be able to curb her behaviour.'

'Which was why you were in such a hurry to marry me—'

Zak was studying her with a strange expression on his face. 'I thought so at the time.'

'But now she's gone—'

Along with the reason for their marriage.

'She has indeed gone,' Zak confirmed with a considerable degree of satisfaction that he didn't even bother to hide. 'And my father has decided that it would be best if she were permitted to live her life away from Kazban.'

'But what about Jamal?'

His mouth tightened. 'Danielle has never been a mother

to Jamal. Her last action before leaving Kazban was to give permission for me to adopt the boy.'

'Oh.' Emily breathed out, surprised by the enormity of his declaration. 'So she isn't going to bother you again—'

'It would appear not.'

Emily licked her lips, suddenly weighed down by a deep depression. 'So finally I get to go home.'

'Ah.' His voice sounded slightly odd in the semi-darkness. 'I'm afraid not.'

'Not?' She stared at him, confused. 'You're still refusing to release me?'

'That's right,' he drawled softly, his masculine tone turning her body to liquid. 'This particular prince is planning to keep you locked up for a bit longer.'

Emily swallowed, achingly aware of his strong fingers still linked through hers. 'How much longer?'

'About one hundred years.'

There was a tense silence while she digested his words. 'Sorry?'

'I love you, Emily,' he said softly, finally releasing her hand, but only so that he could lift her bodily onto his lap. 'And there is no way that anyone is ever going to rescue you from my tower. I am going to keep you there and give you all the babies you've ever wanted.'

Dazed with shock, she curled her fingers into the front of his shirt. 'But you don't believe in love. You believe in marriage contracts and children as a by-product—'

'*Don't* remind me that I said that,' he breathed, and his mouth swooped down on hers. He kissed her until she was breathless and then finally lifted his head with obvious reluctance. 'I was a thoughtless, heartless bastard and I know that I hurt you very badly. I also know how much you've dreamed about a proper family. I want to give you that family, *azîz*. From now on I'm going to be doing everything that the prince in the fairy tale is supposed to do.'

Emily gave a shaky laugh. 'I can't believe you love me.'

'It took me a while to realize it myself,' he confessed ruefully, and she touched his face, still dazed with happiness.

'When did you fall in love with me?'

This was her fairy story and she wanted to be in on every detail.

'It began when you climbed down the palace wall to escape from me,' he drawled, stroking a gentle finger down her cheek. 'It was a first. No woman has ever tried to *escape* from me before. I assumed it was an elaborate act—a very clever trick to attract my attention.' He gave a self-deprecating smile. 'You are a considerable blow to my ego.'

'I just wanted to get home to Peter—'

'And I understand that now, but not then.' He gave a short laugh. 'Your loyalty to your brother does you credit, *azîz*. He is truly fortunate to have you as a sister. I am sure that he will miss you, but he can visit frequently.'

Emily was so happy she couldn't resist teasing him. 'And if I want a divorce?'

'You don't.'

She gave a gasp of amused outrage at his arrogance. 'How do you know? We haven't even discussed my feelings—'

'We have no need to. Your feelings are displayed all over your very beautiful face for the whole world to see,' Zak said dryly, his arms tightening around her. 'You are the most straightforward, uncomplicated woman I have ever met. Unfortunately it took me a long time to realize that but now that I do, I know you love me.'

'How?'

'That night in my bed, you were *so* responsive and I know you wouldn't have been had you not had feelings for me,' he said, his voice smug with masculine satisfaction. 'You love your brother but your dream of a home and a family was too powerful to force you into a marriage that you didn't want. I see that now.'

She smiled, unable to deny what was, after all, the truth. 'Are you always so clever, Your Highness?'

'With you, I have been exceptionally slow,' he groaned, 'but never again. I arrived back at the palace to find Danielle gone and all I could think about was that your brother had repaid the debt and that you no longer had a reason to stay with me.'

'But you said that you knew I loved you—'

'That realization did not come to me until Sharif called to say that you were missing. It was without doubt the worst moment of my life. I flew back here immediately and I vowed that if I found you safe I would *never* let you go again.'

'So what happens now?'

'I assign you a whole army of my most trusted guards so that I can concentrate on my responsibilities knowing that nothing is going to happen to you again. And you get the prince, the palace and the fairy-tale ending, *azîz*.'

And he wrapped his arms around her and kissed her so fiercely that she was left in no doubt as to what the future held.

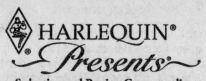

HARLEQUIN® Presents

Seduction and Passion Guaranteed!

Legally wed, but he's never said...
"I love you."

They're...

Wedlocked!

The series
where
marriages are
made in haste...
and love
comes later...

Look out for more Wedlocked! marriage stories
in Harlequin Presents throughout 2005.

Coming in April:
THE BILLION-DOLLAR BRIDE
by Kay Thorpe
#2462

Coming in May:
THE DISOBEDIENT BRIDE
by Helen Bianchin
#2463

Coming in June:
THE MORETTI MARRIAGE
by Catherine Spencer
#2474

www.eHarlequin.com

HPWL2

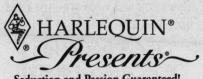

HARLEQUIN®
Presents

Seduction and Passion Guaranteed!

POSSESSED BY THE SHEIKH

An enthralling story set in the desert kingdom of Zuran

After being left stranded in the desert, Katrina was rescued by a robed man on a horse and taken back to his luxury camp. Despite the attraction that sparked between them, the sheikh thought Katrina nothing more than a whore. But there was no way he could leave her to other men. He would have to marry her. And then he discovered— firsthand—that she was a virgin....

On sale April, #2457

Pick up a Harlequin Presents® novel and you will enter a world of spine-tingling passion and provocative, tantalizing romance!

Available wherever Harlequin Books are sold.

www.eHarlequin.com

HPAN

If you enjoyed what you just read,
then we've got an offer you can't resist!

Take 2 bestselling love stories FREE!

Plus get a FREE surprise gift!

Clip this page and mail it to Harlequin Reader Service®

IN U.S.A.	IN CANADA
3010 Walden Ave.	P.O. Box 609
P.O. Box 1867	Fort Erie, Ontario
Buffalo, N.Y. 14240-1867	L2A 5X3

YES! Please send me 2 free Harlequin Presents® novels and my free surprise gift. After receiving them, if I don't wish to receive anymore, I can return the shipping statement marked cancel. If I don't cancel, I will receive 6 brand-new novels every month, before they're available in stores! In the U.S.A., bill me at the bargain price of $3.80 plus 25¢ shipping & handling per book and applicable sales tax, if any*. In Canada, bill me at the bargain price of $4.47 plus 25¢ shipping & handling per book and applicable taxes**. That's the complete price and a savings of at least 10% off the cover prices—what a great deal! I understand that accepting the 2 free books and gift places me under no obligation ever to buy any books. I can always return a shipment and cancel at any time. Even if I never buy another book from Harlequin, the 2 free books and gift are mine to keep forever.

106 HDN DZ7Y
306 HDN DZ7Z

Name	(PLEASE PRINT)	
Address	Apt.#	
City	State/Prov.	Zip/Postal Code

Not valid to current Harlequin Presents® subscribers.

Want to try two free books from another series?
Call 1-800-873-8635 or visit www.morefreebooks.com.

* Terms and prices subject to change without notice. Sales tax applicable in N.Y.
** Canadian residents will be charged applicable provincial taxes and GST.
All orders subject to approval. Offer limited to one per household.
® are registered trademarks owned and used by the trademark owner and or its licensee.

PRES04R   ©2004 Harlequin Enterprises Limited

HARLEQUIN® Presents®

Seduction and Passion Guaranteed!

The O'CONNELLS

by

Sandra Marton

In order to marry, they've got to gamble on love!

Welcome to the world of the wealthy Las Vegas family the O'Connells. Take Keir, Sean, Cullen, Fallon, Megan and Briana into your heart as they begin that most important of life's journeys—a search for deep, passionate, all-enduring love.

Coming in Harlequin Presents®
April 2005 #2458

Briana's story:
THE SICILIAN MARRIAGE
by *Sandra Marton*

Gianni Firelli is used to women trying to get into his bed. So when Briana O'Connell purposely avoids him, she instantly catches his interest. Briana most definitely does not want to be swept off her feet by any man. Or so she thinks, until she meets Gianni....

www.eHarlequin.com   HPTOC

eHARLEQUIN.com

The Ultimate Destination for Women's Fiction

Becoming an eHarlequin.com member is easy, fun and **FREE!** Join today to enjoy great benefits:

- **Super savings** on all our books, including members-only discounts and offers!

- Enjoy **exclusive online reads**—FREE!

- Info, tips and **expert advice** on writing your own romance novel.

- FREE romance **newsletters,** customized by you!

- Find out the latest on your **favorite authors.**

- Enter to win exciting **contests and promotions!**

- Chat with other members in our **community message boards!**

To become a member,
visit www.eHarlequin.com today!

INTMEMB04R